Warrior, sorcerer, and emperor, Elric is driven to call on the Chaos Lord, Arioch, most powerful of all the Dukes of Hell.

And so his first steps are taken on the path of eternal adventure, as the Ship Which Sails Over Land and Sea bears him to the pestilent city of Dhoz-Kam, and his fate leads him through the demonic Shade Gate, where, at the very heart of the Pulsing Cavern two black swords are waiting for their master and their victim . . .

Stormbringer and **Mournblade**.

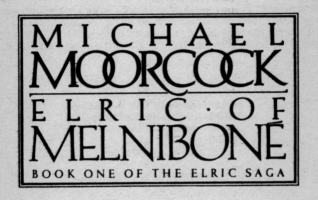

MICHAEL
MOORCOCK
ELRIC · OF
MELNIBONÉ

BOOK ONE OF THE ELRIC SAGA

ACE BOOKS, NEW YORK

You can join the Michael Moorcock fan club! Write to: *Nomads of the Time Streams:* The International Michael Moorcock Appreciation Society, P.O. Box 451048, Atlanta, GA 30345-1048.

A version of this novel, re-edited without the author's permission, was published under the title of *The Dreaming City* by Lancer Books in 1972. The choice of title was also not the author's. This text follows that of the British Edition published in 1972 by Hutchinson & Co., Ltd.

This Ace Book contains the complete
text of the original edition.
It has been completely reset in a typeface
designed for easy reading, and was printed
from new film.

ELRIC OF MELNIBONÉ

An Ace Book / published by arrangement with
the author

PRINTING HISTORY
DAW edition / October 1976
Berkley edition / July 1983
Ace edition / July 1987

ISBN: 0-441-20398-1

Ace Books are published by The Berkley Publishing Group,
200 Madison Avenue, New York, New York 10016.
The name "ACE" and the "A" logo are
trademarks belonging to Charter Communications, Inc.

DEDICATION

To Poul Anderson for *The Broken Sword* and *Three Hearts and Three Lions*. To the late Fletcher Pratt for *The Well of the Unicorn*. To the late Bertolt Brecht for *The Threepenny Opera* which, for obscure reasons, I link with the other books as being one of the chief influences on the first Elric stories.

CONTENTS

BOOK ONE

On the island kingdom of Melniboné all the old rituals are still observed, though the nation's power has waned for five hundred years, and now her way of life is maintained only by her trade with the Young Kingdoms and the fact that the city of Imrryr has become the meeting place of merchants. Are those rituals no longer useful; can the rituals be denied and doom avoided? One who would rule in Emperor Elric's stead prefers to think not. He says that Elric will bring destruction to Melniboné by his refusal to honour all the rituals (Elric honours many). And now opens the tragedy which will close many years from now and precipitate the destruction of this world.

1

A Melancholy King:
A Court Strives to Honour Him

IT IS THE colour of a bleached skull, his flesh; and the long hair which flows below his shoulders is milk-white. From the tapering, beautiful head stare two slanting eyes, crimson and moody, and from the loose sleeves of his yellow gown emerge two slender hands, also the colour of bone, resting on each arm of a seat which has been carved from a single, massive ruby.

The crimson eyes are troubled and sometimes one hand will rise to finger the light helm which sits upon the white locks: a helm made from some dark, greenish alloy and exquisitely moulded into the likeness of a dragon about to take wing. And on the hand which absently caresses the crown there is a ring in which is set a single rare Actorios stone whose core sometimes shifts sluggishly and reshapes itself, as if it were sentient smoke and as restless in its jewelled prison as the young albino on his Ruby Throne.

He looks down the long flight of quartz steps to where his court disports itself, dancing with such delicacy and whispering grace that it might be a court of ghosts. Mentally he debates moral issues and in itself this activity divides him from the great majority of his subjects, for these people are not human.

These are the people of Melniboné, the Dragon Isle, which ruled the world for ten thousand years and has ceased to rule it for less than five hundred years. And they are cruel and clever and to them 'morality' means little more than a proper respect for the traditions of a hundred centuries.

To the young man, four hundred and twenty-eighth in direct line of descent from the first Sorcerer Emperor of Melniboné, their assumptions seem not only arrogant but foolish; it is plain that the Dragon Isle has lost most of her power and will soon be threatened, in another century or two, by a direct conflict with the emerging human nations whom they call, somewhat patronisingly, the Young Kingdoms. Already pirate fleets have made unsuccessful attacks on Imrryr the Beautiful, the Dreaming City, capital of the Dragon Isle of Melniboné.

Yet even the emperor's closest friends refuse to discuss the prospect of Melniboné's fall. They are not pleased when he mentions the idea, considering his remarks not only unthinkable, but also a singular breach of good taste.

So, alone, the emperor broods. He mourns that his father, Sadric the Eighty-Sixth, did not sire more children, for then a more suitable monarch might have been available to take his place on the Ruby Throne. Sadric has been dead a year; whispering a glad welcome to that which came to claim his soul. Through most of his life Sadric had never known another woman than his wife, for the Empress had died bringing her sole thin-blooded issue into the world. But, with Melnibonéan emotions (oddly different from those of the human newcomers), Sadric had loved his wife and had been unable to find pleasure in any other company, even that of the son who had killed her and who was all that was left of her. By magic potions and the chanting of runes, by rare herbs had her son been nurtured, his strength sustained artificially by every art known to the Sorcerer Kings of Melniboné. And he had lived—still lives—thanks to sorcery alone, for he is naturally lassitudinous and, without his drugs, would barely be able to raise his hand from his side through most of a normal day.

If the young emperor has found any advantage in his lifelong weakness it must be in that, perforce, he has read much. Before he was fifteen he had read every book in his father's library, some more than once. His sorcerous powers, learned initially from Sadric, are now greater than any possessed by his ancestors for many a generation. His knowledge of the world beyond the shores of Melniboné is profound, though he has as yet had little direct experience of it. If he wishes he could resurrect the Dragon Isle's former might and rule both his own land and the Young Kingdoms as an invulnerable tyrant. But his reading has also taught him to question the uses to which power is put, to question his motives, to question whether his own power should be used at all, in any cause. His reading has led him to this 'morality', which, still, he barely understands. Thus, to his subjects, he is an enigma and, to some, he is a threat, for he neither thinks nor acts in accordance with their conception of how a true Melnibonéan (and a Melnibonéan emperor, at that) should think and act. His cousin Yyrkoon, for instance, has been heard more than once to voice strong doubts concerning the emperor's right to rule the people of Melniboné. 'This feeble scholar will bring doom to us all,' he said one night to Dyvim Tvar, Lord of the Dragon Caves.

Dyvim Tvar is one of the emperor's few friends and he had duly reported the conversation, but the youth had dismissed the remarks as 'only a trivial treason', whereas any of his ancestors would have rewarded such sentiments with a very slow and exquisite public execution.

The emperor's attitude is further complicated by the fact that Yyrkoon, who is even now making precious little secret of his feelings that he should be emperor, is the brother of Cymoril, a girl whom the albino considers the closest of his friends, and who will one day become his empress.

Down on the mosaic floor of the court Prince Yyrkoon can be seen in all his finest silks and furs, his jewels and his brocades, dancing with a hundred women, all of whom are rumoured to have been mistresses of his at one time or another. His dark features, at once handsome and saturnine, are framed by long black hair, waved and oiled, and his expression, as ever, is sardonic while his bearing is arrogant. The heavy brocade cloak swings this way and that, striking other dancers with some force. He wears it almost as if it is armour or, perhaps, a weapon. Amongst many of the courtiers there is more than a little respect for Prince Yyrkoon. Few resent his arrogance and those who do keep silent, for Yyrkoon is known to be a considerable sorcerer himself. Also his behaviour is what the court expects and welcomes in a Melnibonéan noble; it is what they would welcome in their emperor.

The emperor knows this. He wishes he could please his court as it strives to honour him with its dancing and its wit, but he cannot bring himself to take part in what he privately considers a wearisome and irritating sequence of ritual posturings. In this he is, perhaps, somewhat more arrogant than Yyrkoon who is, at least, a conventional boor.

From the galleries, the music grows louder and more complex as the slaves, specially trained and surgically operated upon to sing but one perfect note each, are stimulated to more passionate efforts. Even the young emperor is moved by the sinister harmony of their song which in few ways resembles anything previously uttered by the human voice. Why should their pain produce such marvellous beauty? he wonders. Or is all beauty created through pain? Is that the secret of great art, both human and Melnibonéan?

The Emperor Elric closes his eyes.

There is a stir in the hall below. The gates have opened and the dancing courtiers cease their motion, drawing back and bowing low as soldiers enter. The soldiers are clad all in light blue, their ornamental helms cast in fantastic shapes, their long, broad-bladed lances decorated with jewelled ribbons. They surround a young woman whose blue dress matches their uniforms and whose bare arms are encircled by five or six bracelets of diamonds, sapphires and gold. Strings of diamonds and sapphires are wound into her hair. Unlike most of the women of the court, her face has no designs painted upon the eyelids or cheekbones. Elric smiles. This is Cymoril. The soldiers are her personal ceremonial guard who, according to tradition, must escort her into the court. They ascend the steps leading to the Ruby Throne. Slowly Elric rises and stretches out his hands.

'Cymoril. I thought you had decided not to grace the court tonight?'

She returns his smile. 'My emperor, I found that I was in the mood for conversation, after all.'

Elric is grateful. She knows that he is bored and she knows, too, that she is one of the few people of Melniboné whose conversation interests him. If protocol allowed, he would offer her the throne, but as it is she must sit on the topmost step at his feet.

'Please sit, sweet Cymoril.' He resumes his place upon the throne and leans forward as she seats herself and looks into his eyes with a mixed expression of humour and tenderness. She speaks softly as her guard withdraws to mingle at the sides of the steps with Elric's own guard. Her voice can be heard only by Elric.

'Would you ride out to the wild region of the island with me tomorrow, my lord?'

'There are matters to which I must give my attention . . .' He is attracted by the idea. It is weeks since he left the city and rode with her, their escort keeping a discreet distance away.

'Are they urgent?'

He shrugs. 'What matters are urgent in Melniboné? After ten thousand years, most problems may be seen in a certain perspective.' His smile is almost a grin, rather like that of a young scholar who plans to play truant from his tutor. 'Very well—early in the morning, we'll leave, before the others are up.'

'The air beyond Imrryr will be clear and sharp. The sun will be warm for the season. The sky will be blue and unclouded.'

Elric laughs. 'Such sorcery you must have worked!'

Cymoril lowers her eyes and traces a pattern on the marble of the dais. 'Well, perhaps a little. I am not without friends among the weakest of the elementals . . .'

Elric stretches down to touch her fine, fair hair. 'Does Yyrkoon know?'

'No.'

Prince Yyrkoon has forbidden his sister to meddle in magical matters. Prince Yyrkoon's friends are only among the darker of the supernatural beings and he knows that they are dangerous to deal with;

thus he assumes that all sorcerous dealings bear a similar element of danger. Besides this, he hates to think that others possess the power that he possesses. Perhaps this is what, in Elric, he hates most of all.

'Let us hope that all Melniboné needs fine weather for tomorrow,' says Elric. Cymoril stares curiously at him. She is still a Melnibonéan. It has not occurred to her that her sorcery might prove unwelcome to some. Then she shrugs her lovely shoulders and touches her lord lightly upon the hand.

'This "guilt",' she says. 'This searching of the conscience. Its purpose is beyond my simple brain.'

'And mine, I must admit. It seems to have no practical function. Yet more than one of our ancestors predicted a change in the nature of our earth. A spiritual as well as a physical change. Perhaps I have glimmerings of this change when I think my stranger, un-Melnibonéan, thoughts?'

The music swells. The music fades. The courtiers dance on, though many eyes are upon Elric and Cymoril as they talk at the top of the dais. There is speculation. When will Elric announce Cymoril as his empress-to-be? Will Elric revive the custom that Sadric dismissed, of sacrificing twelve brides and their bridegrooms to the Lords of Chaos in order to ensure a good marriage for the rulers of Melniboné? It was obvious that Sadric's refusal to allow the custom to continue brought misery upon him and death upon his wife; brought him a sickly son and threatened the very continuity of the monarchy. Elric must revive the custom. Even Elric must fear a repetition of the doom which visited his father. But some say that Elric will do nothing in accordance with tradition and that he threatens not only his own life, but the existence of Melniboné itself and all it stands for. And those who speak thus are often seen to be on good terms with Prince Yyrkoon who dances on, seemingly unaware of their conversation or, indeed, unaware that his sister talks quietly with the cousin who sits on the Ruby Throne; who sits on the edge of the seat, forgetful of his dignity, who exhibits none of the ferocious and disdainful pride which has, in the past, marked virtually every other emperor of Melniboné; who chats animatedly, forgetful that the court is supposed to be dancing for his entertainment.

And then suddenly Prince Yyrkoon freezes in midpirouette and raises his dark eyes to look up at his emperor. In one corner of the hall, Dyvim Tvar's attention is attracted by Yyrkoon's calculated and dramatic posture and the Lord of the Dragon Caves frowns. His hand falls to where his sword would normally be, but no swords are worn at a court ball. Dyvim Tvar looks warily and intently at Prince Yyrkoon as the tall nobleman begins to ascend the stairs to the Ruby Throne. Many eyes follow the emperor's cousin and now hardly anyone dances, though the music grows wilder as the masters of the music slaves goad their charges to even greater exertions.

Elric looks up to see Yyrkoon standing one step below that on which Cymoril sits. Yyrkoon makes a bow which is subtly insulting.

'I present myself to my emperor,' he says.

2

An Upstart Prince:
He Confronts His Cousin

'AND HOW DO you enjoy the ball, cousin?' Elric asked, aware that Yyrkoon's melodramatic presentation had been designed to catch him off-guard and, if possible, humiliate him. 'Is the music to your taste?'

Yyrkoon lowered his eyes and let his lips form a secret little smile. 'Everything is to my taste, my liege. But what of yourself? Does something displease you? You do not join the dance.'

Elric raised one pale finger to his chin and stared at Yyrkoon's hidden eyes. 'I enjoy the dance, cousin, nonetheless. Surely it is possible to take pleasure in the pleasure of others?'

Yyrkoon seemed genuinely astonished. His eyes opened fully and met Elric's. Elric felt a slight shock and then turned his own gaze away, indicating the music galleries with a languid hand. 'Or perhaps it is the pain of others which brings me pleasure. Fear not, for my sake, cousin. I am pleased. I am pleased. You may dance on, assured that your emperor enjoys the ball.'

But Yyrkoon was not to be diverted from his object. 'Surely, if his subjects are not to go away saddened and troubled that they have not pleased their ruler, the emperor should demonstrate his enjoyment . . .?'

'I would remind you, cousin,' said Elric quietly, 'that the emperor has no duty to his subjects at all, save to rule them. Their duty is to him. That is the tradition of Melniboné.'

Yyrkoon had not expected Elric to use such arguments against him, but he rallied with his next retort. 'I agree, my lord. The emperor's duty is to rule his subjects. Perhaps that is why so many of them do not, themselves, enjoy the ball as much as they might.'

'I do not follow you, cousin.'

Cymoril had risen and stood with her hands clenched on the step above her brother. She was tense and anxious, worried by her brother's bantering tone, his disdainful bearing.

'Yyrkoon . . .' she said.

He acknowledged her presence. 'Sister. I see you share our emperor's reluctance to dance.'

'Yyrkoon,' she murmured, 'you are going too far. The emperor is tolerant, but . . .'

'Tolerant? Or is he careless? Is he careless of the traditions of our great race? Is he contemptuous of that race's pride?'

Dyvim Tvar was now mounting the steps. It was plain that he, too, sensed that Yyrkoon had chosen this moment to test Elric's power.

Cymoril was aghast. She said urgently: 'Yyrkoon. If you would live . . .'

'I would not care to live if the soul of Melniboné perished. And the guardianship of our nation's soul is the responsibility of the emperor. And what if we should have an emperor who failed in that responsibility? An emperor who was weak? An emperor who cared nothing for the greatness of the Dragon Isle and its folk?'

'A hypothetical question, cousin.' Elric had recovered his composure and his voice was an icy drawl. 'For such an emperor has never sat upon the Ruby Throne and such an emperor never shall.'

Dyvim Tvar came up, touching Yyrkoon on the shoulder. 'Prince, if you value your dignity and your life . . .'

Elric raised his hand. 'There is no need for that, Dyvim Tvar. Prince Yyrkoon merely entertains us with an intellectual debate. Fearing that I was bored by the music and the dance—which I am not—he thought he would provide the subject for a stimulating discourse. I am certain that we are most stimulated, Prince Yyrkoon.' Elric allowed a patronising warmth to colour his last sentence.

Yyrkoon flushed with anger and bit his lip.

'But go on, dear cousin Yyrkoon,' Elric said. 'I am interested. Enlarge further on your argument.'

Yyrkoon looked around him, as if for support. But all his supporters were on the floor of the hall. Only Elric's friends, Dyvim Tvar and Cymoril, were nearby. Yet Yyrkoon knew that his supporters were hearing every word and that he would lose face if he did not retaliate. Elric could tell that Yyrkoon would have preferred to have retired from this confrontation and choose another day and another ground on which to continue the battle, but that was not possible. Elric, himself, had no wish to continue the foolish banter which was, no matter how disguised, a little better than the quarrelling of two little girls over who should play with the slaves first. He decided to make an end to it.

Yyrkoon began: 'Then let me suggest that an emperor who was physically weak might also be weak in his will to rule as befitted . . .'

And Elric raised his hand. 'You have done

enough, dear cousin. More than enough. You have
wearied yourself with this conversation when you
would have preferred to dance. I am touched by
your concern. But now I, too, feel weariness steal
upon me.' Elric signaled for his old servant Tanglebones who stood on the far side of the throne dais,
amongst the soldiers. 'Tanglebones! My cloak.'

Elric stood up. 'I thank you again for your
thoughtfulness, cousin.' He addressed the court in
general. 'I was entertained. Now I retire.'

Tanglebones brought the cloak of white fox fur
and placed it around his master's shoulders. Tanglebones was very old and much taller than Elric,
though his back was stooped and all his limbs
seemed knotted and twisted back on themselves, like
the limbs of a strong, old tree.

Elric walked across the dais and through the door
which opened onto a corridor which led to his private apartments.

Yyrkoon was left fuming. He whirled round on
the dais and opened his mouth as if to address the
watching courtiers. Some, who did not support
him, were smiling quite openly. Yyrkoon clenched
his fists at his sides and glowered. He glared at
Dyvim Tvar and opened his thin lips to speak.
Dyvim Tvar coolly returned the glare, daring
Yyrkoon to say more.

Then Yrykoon flung back his head so that the
locks of his hair, all curled and oiled, swayed against
his back. And Yyrkoon laughed.

The harsh sound filled the hall. The music
stopped. The laughter continued.

Yyrkoon stepped up so that he stood on the dais.
He dragged his heavy cloak round him so that it engulfed his body.

Cymoril came forward. 'Yyrkoon, please do

not . . .' He pushed her back with a motion of his shoulder.

Yyrkoon walked stiffly towards the Ruby Throne. It became plain that he was about to seat himself in it and thus perform one of the most traitorous actions possible in the code of Melniboné. Cymoril ran the few steps to him and pulled at his arm.

Yyrkoon's laughter grew. 'It is Yyrkoon they would wish to see on the Ruby Throne,' he told his sister. She gasped and looked in horror at Dyvim Tvar whose face was grim and angry.

Dyvim Tvar signed to the guards and suddenly there were two ranks of armoured men between Yyrkoon and the throne.

Yyrkoon glared back at the Lord of the Dragon Caves. 'You had best hope you perish with your master,' he hissed.

'This guard of honour will escort you from the hall,' Dyvim Tvar said evenly. 'We were all stimulated by your conversation this evening, Prince Yyrkoon.'

Yyrkoon paused, looked about him, then relaxed. He shrugged. 'There's time enough. If Elric will not abdicate, then he must be deposed.'

Cymoril's slender body was rigid. Her eyes blazed. She said to her brother:

'If you harm Elric in any way, I will slay you myself, Yyrkoon.'

He raised his tapering eyebrows and smiled. At that moment he seemed to hate his sister even more than he hated his cousin. 'Your loyalty to that creature has ensured your own doom, Cymoril. I would rather you died than that you should give birth to any progeny of his. I will not have the blood of our house diluted, tainted—even touched—by his blood. Look to your own life, sister, before you threaten mine.'

And he stormed down the steps, pushing through those who came up to congratulate him. He knew that he had lost and the murmurs of his sycophants only irritated him further.

The great doors of the hall crashed together and closed. Yyrkoon was gone from the hall.

Dyvim Tvar raised both his arms. 'Dance on, courtiers. Pleasure yourselves with all that the hall provides. It is what will please the emperor most.'

But it was plain there would be little more dancing done tonight. Courtiers were already deep in conversation as, excitedly, they debated the events.

Dyvim Tvar turned to Cymoril. 'Elric refuses to understand the danger, Princess Cymoril. Yyrkoon's ambition could bring disaster to all of us.'

'Including Yyrkoon.' Cymoril sighed.

'Aye, including Yyrkoon. But how can we avoid this, Cymoril, if Elric will not give orders for your brother's arrest?'

'He believes that such as Yyrkoon should be allowed to say what they please. It is part of his philosophy. I can barely understand it, but it seems integral to his whole belief. If he destroys Yyrkoon, he destroys the basis on which his logic works. That at any rate, Dragon Master, is what he has tried to explain to me.'

Dyvim Tvar sighed and he frowned. Though unable to understand Elric, he was afraid that he could sometimes sympathise with Yyrkoon's viewpoint. At least Yyrkoon's motives and arguments were relatively straightforward. He knew Elric's character too well, however, to believe that Elric acted from weakness or lassitude. The paradox was that Elric tolerated Yyrkoon's treachery because he was strong, because he had the power to destroy Yyrkoon whenever he cared. And Yyrkoon's own character was such that he must constantly be testing that strength of Elric's, for he knew instinctively that if Elric did weaken and order him slain, then he would have won. It was a complicated situation and Dyvim Tvar dearly wished that he was not embroiled in it. But his loyalty to the royal line of Melniboné was strong and his personal loyalty to Elric was great. He considered the idea of having Yyrkoon secretly assassinated, but he knew that such a plan would almost certainly come to nothing. Yyrkoon was a sorcerer of immense power and doubtless would be forewarned of any attempt on his life.

'Princess Cymoril,' said Dyvim Tvar, 'I can only pray that your brother swallows so much of his rage that it eventually poisons him.'

'I will join you in that prayer, Lord of the Dragon Caves.'

Together, they left the hall.

3

Riding Through the Morning:
A Moment of Tranquillity

THE LIGHT OF the early morning touched the tall towers of Imrryr and made them scintillate. Each tower was of a different hue; there were a thousand soft colours. There were rose pinks and pollen yellows, there were purples and pale greens, mauves and browns and oranges, hazy blues, whites and powdery golds, all lovely in the sunlight. Two riders left the Dreaming City behind them and rode away from the walls, over the green turf towards a pine forest where, among the shadowy trunks, a little of the night seemed to remain. Squirrels were stirring and foxes crept homeward; birds were singing and forest flowers opened their petals and filled the air with delicate scent. A few insects wandered sluggishly aloft. The contrast between life in the nearby city and this lazy rusticity was very great and seemed to mirror some of the contrasts existing in the mind of at least one of the riders who now dismounted and led his horse, walking knee-deep through a mass of blue flowers. The other rider, a girl, brought her own horse to a halt but did not dismount. Instead, she leaned casually on her high Melnibonéan pommel and smiled at the man, her lover.

'Elric? Would you stop so near to Imrryr?'

He smiled back at her, over his shoulder. 'For the moment. Our flight was hasty. I would collect my thoughts before we ride on.'

'How did you sleep last night?'

'Well enough, Cymoril, though I must have dreamed without knowing it, for there were—there were little intimations in my head when I awoke. But then, the meeting with Yyrkoon was not pleasant . . .'

'Do you think he plots to use sorcery against you?'

Elric shrugged. 'I would know if he brought a large sorcery against me. And he knows my power. I doubt if he would dare employ wizardry.'

'He has reason to believe you might not use your power. He has worried at your personality for so long—is there not a danger he will begin to worry at your skills? Testing your sorcery as he has tested your patience?'

Elric frowned. 'Yes, I suppose there is that danger. But not yet, I should have thought.'

'He will not be happy until you are destroyed, Elric.'

'Or is destroyed himself, Cymoril.' Elric stooped and picked one of the flowers. He smiled. 'Your brother is inclined to absolutes, is he not? How the weak hate weakness.'

Cymoril took his meaning. She dismounted and came towards him. Her thin gown matched, almost perfectly, the colour of the flowers through which she moved. He handed her the flower and she accepted it, touching its petals with her perfect lips. 'And how the strong hate strength, my love. Yyrkoon is my kin and yet I give you this advice— use your strength against him.'

'I could not slay him. I have not the right.' Elric's face fell into familiar, brooding lines.

'You could exile him.'

'Is not exile the same as death to a Melnibonéan?'

'You, yourself, have talked of travelling in the lands of the Young Kingdoms.'

Elric laughed somewhat bitterly. 'But perhaps I am not a true Melnibonéan. Yyrkoon has said as much—and others echo his thoughts.'

'He hates you because you are contemplative. Your father was contemplative and no one denied that he was a fitting emperor.'

'My father chose not to put the results of his contemplation into his personal actions. He ruled as an emperor should. Yyrkoon, I must admit, would also rule as an emperor should. He, too, has the opportunity to make Melniboné great again. If he were emperor, he would embark on a campaign of conquest to restore our trade to its former volume, to extend our power across the earth. And that is what the majority of our folk would wish. Is it my right to deny that wish?'

'It is your right to do what you think, for you are the emperor. All who are loyal to you think as I do.'

'Perhaps their loyalty is misguided. Perhaps Yyrkoon is right and I will betray that loyalty, bring doom to the Dragon Isle?' His moody, crimson eyes looked directly into hers. 'Perhaps I should have died as I left my mother's womb. Then Yyrkoon would have become emperor. Has Fate been thwarted?'

'Fate is never thwarted. What has happened has happened because Fate willed it thus—if, indeed, there is such a thing as Fate and if men's actions are not merely a response to other men's actions.'

Elric drew a deep breath and offered her an expression tinged with irony. 'Your logic leads you close to heresy, Cymoril, if we are to believe the traditions of Melniboné. Perhaps it would be better if you forgot your friendship with me.'

She laughed. 'You begin to sound like my brother. Are you testing my love for you, my lord?'

He began to remount his horse. 'No, Cymoril, but I would advise you to test your love yourself, for I sense there is tragedy implicit in our love.'

As she swung herself back into her saddle she smiled and shook her head. 'You see doom in all things. Can you not accept the good gifts granted you? They are few enough, my lord.'

'Aye. I'll agree with that.'

They turned in their saddles, hearing hoofbeats behind them. Some distance away they saw a company of yellow-clad horsemen riding about in confusion. It was their guard, which they had left behind, wishing to ride alone.

'Come!' cried Elric. 'Through the woods and over yonder hill and they'll never find us!'

They spurred their steeds through the sun-speared wood and up the steep sides of the hill beyond, racing down the other side and away across a plain where noidel bushes grew, their lush, poison fruit glimmering a purplish blue, a night-colour which even the light of day could not disperse. There were many such peculiar berries and herbs on Melniboné and it was to some of them that Elric owed his life. Others were used for sorcerous potions and had been sown generations before by Elric's ancestors. Now few Melnibonéans left Imrryr even to collect these harvests. Only slaves visited the greater part of the island, seeking the roots and the shrubs which made men dream monstrous and magnificent dreams, for it was in their dreams that the nobles of Melniboné found most of their pleasures; they had ever been a moody, inward-looking race and it was for this quality that Imrryr had come to be named the Dreaming City. There, even the meanest slaves

chewed berries to bring them oblivion and thus were
easily controlled, for they came to depend on their
dreams. Only Elric himself refused such drugs, perhaps because he required so many others simply to
ensure his remaining alive.

The yellow-clad guards were lost behind them and
once across the plain where the noidel bushes grew
they slowed their flight and came at length to cliffs
and then the sea.

The sea shone brightly and languidly washed the
white beaches below the cliffs. Seabirds wheeled in
the clear sky and their cries were distant, serving
only to emphasise the sense of peace which both
Elric and Cymoril now had. In silence the lovers
guided their horses down steep paths to the shore
and there they tethered the steeds and began to walk
across the sand, their hair—his white, hers jet
black—waving in the wind which blew from the
east.

They found a great, dry cave which caught the
sounds the sea made and replied in a whispering
echo. They removed their silken garments and made
love tenderly in the shadows of the cave. They lay in
each other's arms as the day warmed and the wind
dropped. Then they went to bathe in the waters, filling the empty sky with their laughter.

When they were dry and were dressing themselves
they noticed a darkening of the horizon and Elric
said: 'We shall be wet again before we return to Imrryr. No matter how fast we ride, the storm will catch
us.'

'Perhaps we should remain in the cave until it is
past?' she suggested, coming close and holding her
soft body against him.

'No,' he said. 'I must return soon, for there are
potions in Imrryr I must take if my body is to retain
its strength. An hour or two longer and I shall begin

to weaken. You have seen me weak before, Cymoril.'

She stroked his face and her eyes were sympathetic. 'Aye. I've seen you weak before, Elric. Come, let's find the horses.'

By the time they reached the horses the sky was grey overhead and full of boiling blackness not far away in the east. They heard the grumble of thunder and the crash of lightning. The sea was threshing as if infected by the sky's hysteria. The horses snorted and pawed at the sand, anxious to return. Even as Elric and Cymoril climbed into their saddles large spots of rain began to fall on their heads and spread over their cloaks.

Then, suddenly, they were riding at full tilt back to Imrryr while the lightning flashed around them and the thunder roared like a furious giant, like some great old Lord of Chaos attempting to break through, unbidden, into the Realm of Earth.

Cymoril glanced at Elric's pale face, illuminated for a moment by a flash of sky-fire, and she felt a chill come upon her then and the chill had nothing to do with the wind or the rain, for it seemed to her in that second that the gentle scholar she loved had been transformed by the elements into a hell-driven demon, into a monster with barely a semblance of humanity. His crimson eyes had flared from the whiteness of his skull like the very flames of the Higher Hell; his hair had been whipped upward so that it had become the crest of a sinister warhelm and, by a trick of the stormlight, his mouth had seemed twisted in a mixture of rage and agony.

And suddenly Cymoril knew.

She knew, profoundly, that their morning's ride was the last moment of peace the two of them would ever experience again. The storm was a sign from the gods themselves—a warning of storms to come.

She looked again at her lover. Elric was laughing.
He had turned his face upward so that the warm
rain fell upon it, so that the water splashed into his
open mouth. The laughter was the easy, unsophisti-
cated laughter of a happy child.

Cymoril tried to laugh back, but then she had to
turn her face away so that he should not see it. For
Cymoril had begun to weep.

She was weeping still when Imrryr came in sight—
a black and grotesque silhouette against a line of
brightness which was the as yet untainted western
horizon.

4

Prisoners: Their Secrets Are Taken from Them

THE MEN IN yellow armour saw Elric and Cymoril as the two approached the smallest of the eastern gates.

'They have found us at last,' smiled Elric through the rain, 'but somewhat belatedly, eh, Cymoril?'

Cymoril, still embattled with her sense of doom, merely nodded and tried to smile in reply.

Elric took this as an expression of disappointment, nothing more, and called to his guards: 'Ho, men! Soon we shall all be dry again!'

But the captain of the guard rode up urgently, crying: 'My lord emperor is needed at Monshanjik Tower where spies are held.'

'Spies?'

'Aye, my lord.' The man's face was pale. Water cascaded from his helm and darkened his thin cloak. His horse was hard to control and kept sidestepping through pools of water, which had gathered wherever the road was in disrepair. 'Caught in the maze this morning. Southern barbarians, by their chequered dress. We are holding them until the emperor himself can question them.'

Elric waved his hand. 'Then lead on, captain. Let's see the brave fools who dare Melniboné's sea-maze.'

The Tower of Monshanjik had been named for the wizard-architect who had designed the sea-maze millennia before. The maze was the only means of reaching the great harbour of Imrryr and its secrets had been carefully guarded, for it was their greatest protection against sudden attack. The maze was complicated and pilots had to be specially trained to steer ships through it. Before the maze had been built, the harbour had been a kind of inland lagoon, fed by the sea which swept in through a system of natural caverns in the towering cliff which rose between lagoon and ocean. There were five separate routes through the sea-maze and any individual pilot knew but one. In the outer wall of the cliff there were five entrances. Here Young Kingdom ships waited until a pilot came aboard. Then one of the gates to one of the entrances would be lifted, all aboard the ship would be blindfolded and sent below save for the oar-master and the steersman who would also be masked in heavy steel helms so that they could see nothing, do nothing but obey the complicated instructions of the pilot. And if a Young Kingdom ship should fail to obey any of those instructions and should crush itself against the rock walls, well Melniboné did not mourn for it and any survivors from the crew would be taken as slaves. All who sought to trade with the Dreaming City understood the risks, but scores of merchants came every month to dare the dangers of the maze and trade their own poor goods for the splendid riches of Melniboné.

The Tower of Monshanjik stood overlooking the harbour and the massive mole which jutted out into the middle of the lagoon. It was a sea-green tower and was squat compared with most of those in Imrryr, though still a beautiful and tapering construction, with wide windows so that the whole of the harbour could be seen from it. From Monshanjik Tower most of the business of the harbour was done and in its lower cellars were kept any prisoners who had broken any of the myriad rules governing the functioning of the harbour. Leaving Cymoril to return to the palace with a guard, Elric entered the tower, riding through the great archway at the base, scattering not a few merchants who were waiting for permission to begin their bartering, for the whole of the ground floor was full of sailors, merchants and Melnibonéan officials engaged in the business of trade, though it was not here that the actual wares were displayed. The great echoing babble of a thousand voices engaged in a thousand separate aspects of bargaining slowly stilled as Elric and his guard rode arrogantly through to another dark arch at the far end of the hall. This arch opened onto a ramp which sloped and curved down into the bowels of the tower.

Down this ramp clattered the horsemen, passing slaves, servants and officials who stepped hastily aside, bowing low as they recognised the emperor. Great brands illuminated the tunnel, guttering and smoking and casting distorted shadows onto the smooth, obsidian walls. A chill was in the air now, and a dampness, for water washed about the outer walls below the quays of Imrryr. And still the emperor rode on and still the ramp struck lower through the glassy rock. And then a wave of heat rose to meet them and shifting light could be seen ahead and they passed into a chamber that was full of smoke and the scent of fear. From the low ceiling hung chains and from eight of the chains, swinging by their feet, hung four people. Their clothes had been torn from them, but their bodies were clothed in blood from tiny wounds, precise but severe, made by the artist who stood, scalpel in hand, surveying his handiwork.

The artist was tall and very thin, almost like a skeleton in his stained, white garments. His lips were thin, his eyes were slits, his fingers were thin, his hair was thin and the scalpel he held was thin, too, almost invisible save when it flashed in the light from the fire which erupted from a pit on the far side of the cavern. The artist was named Doctor Jest and the art he practised was a performing art rather than a creative one (though he could argue otherwise with some conviction): the art of drawing secrets from those who kept them. Doctor Jest was the Chief Interrogator of Melniboné. He turned sinuously as Elric entered, the scalpel held between the thin thumb and the thin forefinger of his right hand; he stood poised and expectant, almost like a dancer, and then bowed from the waist.

'My sweet emperor!' His voice was thin. It rushed from his thin throat as if bent on escape and one was inclined to wonder if one had heard the words at all, so quickly had they come and gone.

'Doctor. Are these the southlanders caught this morning?'

'Indeed they are, my lord.' Another sinuous bow. 'For your pleasure.'

Coldly Elric inspected the prisoners. He felt no sympathy for them. They were spies. Their actions had led them to this pass. They had known what would happen to them if caught. But one of them was a boy and another a woman, it appeared, though they writhed so in their chains it was quite difficult to tell at first. It seemed a shame. Then the woman snapped what remained of her teeth at him and hissed: 'Demon!' And Elric stepped back, saying:

'Have they informed you of what they were doing in our maze, doctor?'

'They still tantalise me with hints. They have a fine sense of drama. I appreciate that. They are here, I would say, to map a route through the maze which a force of raiders might then follow. But they have so far withheld the details. That is the game. We all understand how it must be played.'

'And when will they tell you, Doctor Jest?'

'Oh, very soon, my lord.'

'It would be best to know if we are to expect attackers. The sooner we know, the less time we shall lose dealing with the attack when it comes. Do you not agree, doctor?'

'I do, my lord.'

'Very well.' Elric was irritated by this break in his day. It had spoiled the pleasure of the ride, it had brought him face to face with his duties too quickly.

Doctor Jest returned to his charges and, reaching out with his free hand, expertly seized the genitals of one of the male prisoners. The scalpel flashed. There was a groan. Doctor Jest tossed something onto the fire. Elric sat in the chair prepared for him. He was bored rather than disgusted by the rituals attendant upon the gathering of information and the discordant screams, the clash of the chains, the thin whisperings of Doctor Jest, all served to ruin the feeling of well-being he had retained even as he reached the chamber. But it was one of his kingly duties to attend such rituals and attend this one he must until the information was presented to him and he could congratulate his Chief Interrogator and issue orders as to the means of dealing with any attack and even when that was over he must confer with admirals and with generals, probably through the rest of the night, choosing between arguments, deciding on the deposition of men and ships. With a poorly disguised yawn he leaned back and watched

as Doctor Jest ran fingers and scalpel, tongue, tongs
and pincers over the bodies. He was soon thinking
of other matters: philosophical problems which he
had still failed to resolve.

It was not that Elric was inhumane; it was that he
was, still, a Melnibonéan. He had been used to such
sights since childhood. He could not have saved the
prisoners, even if he had desired, without going
against every tradition of the Dragon Isle. And in
this case it was a simple matter of a threat being met
by the best methods available. He had become used
to shutting off those feelings which conflicted with
his duties as emperor. If there had been any point in
freeing the four who danced now at Doctor Jest's
pleasure he would have freed them, but there was no
point and the four would have been astonished if
they had received any other treatment than this.
Where moral decisions were concerned Elric was, by
and large, practical. He would make his decision in
the context of what action he could take. In this
case, he could take no action. Such a reaction had
become second nature to him. His desire was not to
reform Melniboné but to reform himself, not to ini-
tiate action but to know the best way of responding
to the actions of others. Here, the decision was easy
to make. A spy was an aggressor. One defended oneself against aggressors in the best possible way. The
methods employed by Doctor Jest were the best
methods.

'My lord?'

Absently, Elric looked up.

'We have the information now, my lord.' Doctor
Jest's thin voice whispered across the chamber. Two
sets of chains were now empty and slaves were gathering things up from the floor and flinging them on
the fire. The two remaining shapeless lumps reminded Elric of meat carefully prepared by a chef.

One of the lumps still quivered a little, but the other was still.

Doctor Jest slid his instruments into a thin case he carried in a pouch at his belt. His white garments were almost completely covered in stains.

'It seems there have been other spies before these,' Doctor Jest told his master. 'These came merely to confirm the route. If they do not return in time, the barbarians will still sail.'

'But surely they will know that we expect them?' Elric said.

'Probably not, my lord. Rumours have been spread amongst the Young Kingdom merchants and sailors that four spies were seen in the maze and were speared—slain whilst trying to escape.'

'I see.' Elric frowned. 'Then our best plan will be to lay a trap for the raiders.'

'Aye, my lord.'

'You know the route they have chosen?'

'Aye, my lord.'

Elric turned to one of his guards. 'Have messages sent to all our generals and admirals. What's the hour?'

'The hour of sunset is just past, my liege.'

'Tell them to assemble before the Ruby Throne at two hours past sunset.'

Wearily, Elric rose. 'You have done well, as usual, Doctor Jest.'

The thin artist bowed low, seeming to fold himself in two. A thin and somewhat unctuous sigh was his reply.

5

A Battle: The King Proves His War-Skill

YYRKOON WAS THE first to arrive, all clad in martial finery, accompanied by two massive guards, each holding one of the prince's ornate war-banners.

'My emperor!' Yyrkoon's shout was proud and disdainful. 'Would you let me command the warriors? It will relieve you of that care when, doubtless, you have many other concerns with which to occupy your time.'

Elric replied impatiently: 'You are most thoughtful, Prince Yyrkoon, but fear not for me. I shall command the armies and the navies of Melniboné, for that is the duty of the emperor.'

Yyrkoon glowered and stepped to one side as Dyvim Tvar, Lord of the Dragon Caves, entered. He had no guard whatsoever with him and it seemed he had dressed hastily. He carried his helmet under his arm.

'My emperor—I bring news of the dragons . . .'

'I thank you, Dyvim Tvar, but wait until all my commanders are assembled and impart that news to them, too.'

Dyvim Tvar bowed and went to stand on the opposite side of the hall to that on which Prince Yyrkoon stood.

Gradually the warriors arrived until a score of great captains waited at the foot of the steps which led to the Ruby Throne where Elric sat. Elric himself still wore the clothes in which he had gone riding that morning. He had not had time to change and had until a little while before been consulting maps of the mazes—maps which only he could read and which, at normal times, were hidden by magical means from any who might attempt to find them.

'Southlanders would steal Imrryr's wealth and slay us all,' Elric began. 'They believe they have found a way through our sea-maze. A fleet of a hundred warships sails on Melniboné even now. Tomorrow it will wait below the horizon until dusk, then it will sail to the maze and enter. By midnight it expects to reach the harbour and to have taken the Dreaming City before dawn. Is that possible, I wonder?'

'No!' Many spoke the single word.

'No.' Elric smiled. 'But how shall we best enjoy this little war they offer us?'

Yyrkoon, as ever, was first to shout. 'Let us go to meet them now, with dragons and with battle-barges. Let us pursue them to their own land and take their war to them. Let us attack their nations and burn their cities! Let us conquer them and thus ensure our own security!'

Dyvim Tvar spoke up again:

'No dragons,' he said.

'What?' Yyrkoon whirled. 'What?'

'No dragons, prince. They will not be awakened. The dragons sleep in their caverns, exhausted by their last engagement on your behalf.'

'Mine?'

'You would use them in our conflict with the Vilmirian pirates. I told you that I would prefer to

save them for a larger engagement. But you flew
them against the pirates and you burned their little
boats and now the dragons sleep.'

Yyrkoon glowered. He looked up at Elric. 'I did
not expect . . .'

Elric raised his hand. 'We need not use our dragons until such a time as we really need them. This
attack from the southlander fleet is nothing. But we
will conserve our strength if we bide our time. Let
them think we are unready. Let them enter the maze.
Once the whole hundred are through, we close in,
blocking off all routes in or out of the maze.
Trapped, they will be crushed by us.'

Yyrkoon looked pettishly at his feet, evidently
wishing he could think of some flaw in the plan.
Tall, old Admiral Magum Colim in his sea-green armour stepped forward and bowed. 'The golden
battle-barges of Imrryr are ready to defend their
city, my liege. It will take time, however, to manoeuvre them into position. It is doubtful if all will
fit into the maze at once.'

'Then sail some of them out now and hide them
around the coast, so that they can wait for any survivors that may escape our attack,' Elric instructed
him.

'A useful plan, my liege.' Magum Colim bowed
and sank back into the crowd of his peers.

The debate continued for some time and then they
were ready and about to leave. But then Prince
Yyrkoon bellowed once more:

'I repeat my offer to the emperor. His person is
too valuable to risk in battle. My person—it is
worthless. Let me command the warriors of both
land and sea while the emperor may remain at the
palace, untroubled by the battle, confident that it
will be won and the southlanders trounced—
perhaps there is a book he wishes to finish?'

Elric smiled. 'Again I thank you for your concern, Prince Yyrkoon. But an emperor must exercise his body as well as his mind. I will command the warriors tomorrow.'

When Elric arrived back at his apartments it was to discover that Tanglebones had already laid out his heavy, black wargear. Here was the armour which had served a hundred Melnibonéan emperors; an armour which was forged by sorcery to give it a strength unequalled on the Realm of Earth, which could, so rumour went, even withstand the bite of the mythical runeblades, Stormbringer and Mournblade, which had been wielded by the wickedest of Melniboné's many wicked rulers before being seized by the Lords of the Higher Worlds and hidden forever in a realm where even those Lords might rarely venture.

The face of the tangled man was full of joy as he touched each piece of armour, each finely balanced weapon, with his long, gnarled fingers. His seamed face looked up to regard Elric's care-ravaged features. 'Oh, my lord! Oh, my king! Soon you will know the joy of the fight!'

'Aye, Tanglebones—and let us hope it will be a joy.'

'I taught you all the skills—the art of the sword and the poignard—the art of the bow—the art of the spear, both mounted and on foot. And you learned well, for all they say you are weak. Save one, there's no better swordsman in Melniboné.'

'Prince Yyrkoon could be better than me,' Elric said reflectively. 'Could he not?'

'I said "save one", my lord.'

'And Yyrkoon is that one. Well, one day perhaps we'll be able to test the matter. I'll bathe before I don all that metal.'

'Best make speed, master. From what I hear, there is much to do.'

'And I'll sleep after I've bathed.' Elric smiled at

his old friend's consternation. 'It will be better thus, for I cannot personally direct the barges into position. I am needed to command the fray—and that I will do better when I've rested.'

'If you think it good, lord king, then it is good.'

'And you are astonished. You are too eager, Tanglebones, to get me into all that stuff and see me strut about in it as if I were Arioch himself . . .'

Tanglebones's hand flew to his mouth as if he had spoken the words, not his master, and he was trying to block them. His eyes widened.

Elric laughed. 'You think I speak bold heresies, eh? Well, I've spoken worse without any ill befalling me. On Melniboné, Tanglebones, the emperors control the demons, not the reverse.'

'So you say, my liege.'

'It is the truth.' Elric swept from the room, calling for his slaves. The war-fever filled him and he was jubilant.

Now he was in all his black gear: the massive breastplate, the padded jerkin, the long greaves, the mail gauntlets. At his side was a five-foot broadsword which, it was said, had belonged to a human hero called Aubec. Resting on the deck against the golden rail of the bridge was the great round warboard, his shield, bearing the sign of the swooping dragon. And a helm was on his head; a black helm, with a dragon's head craning over the peak, and dragon's wings flaring backward above it, and a dragon's tail curling down the back. All the helm was black, but within the helm there was a white shadow from which glared two crimson orbs, and from the sides of the helm strayed wisps of milk-white hair, almost like smoke escaping from a burning building. And, as the helm turned in what little light came from the lantern hanging at the base of the mainmast, the white shadow sharpened to reveal features—fine, handsome features—a straight nose, curved lips, up-slanting eyes. The face of Emperor Elric of Melniboné peered into the gloom of the maze as he listened for the first sounds of the sea-raider's approach.

He stood on the high bridge of the great golden battle-barge which, like all its kind, resembled a floating ziggurat equipped with masts and sails and oars and catapults. The ship was called *The Son of the Pyaray* and it was the flagship of the fleet. The Grand Admiral Magum Colim stood beside Elric. Like Dyvim Tvar, the admiral was one of Elric's few close friends. He had known Elric all his life and had encouraged him to learn all he could concerning the running of fighting ships and fighting fleets. Privately Magum Colim might fear that Elric was too scholarly and introspective to rule Melniboné, but he accepted Elric's right to rule and was made angry and impatient by the talk of the likes of Yyrkoon. Prince Yyrkoon was also aboard the flagship, though at this moment he was below, inspecting the war-engines.

The Son of the Pyaray lay at anchor in a huge grotto, one of hundreds built into the walls of the maze when the maze itself was built, and designed for just this purpose—to hide a battle-barge. There was just enough height for the masts and enough width for the oars to move freely. Each of the golden battle-barges was equipped with banks of oars, each bank containing between twenty and thirty oars on either side. The banks were four, five or six decks high and, as in the case of *The Son of the Pyaray,* might have three independent steering systems, fore and aft. Being armoured all in gold, the ships were virtually indestructible, and, for all their massive size, they could move swiftly and manoeuvre delicately when occasion demanded. It was not the first time they had waited for their enemies in these grottoes. It would not be the last (though when next they waited it would be in greatly different circumstances).

The battle-barges of Melniboné were rarely seen on the open seas these days, but once they had sailed the oceans of the world like fearsome floating mountains of gold and they had brought terror whenever they were sighted. The fleet had been larger then, comprising hundreds of craft. Now there were less than forty ships. But forty would suffice. Now, in damp darkness, they awaited their enemies.

Listening to the hollow slap of the water against the sides of the ship, Elric wished that he had been able to conceive a better plan than this. He was sure that this one would work, but he regretted the waste of lives, both Melnibonéan and barbarian. It would have been beter if some way could have been devised of frightening the barbarians away rather than trapping them in the sea-maze. The southlander fleet was not the first to have been attracted by Imrryr's fabulous wealth. The southlander crews were not the first to entertain the belief that the Melnibonéans, because they never now ventured far from the Dreaming City, had become decadent and unable to defend their treasures. And so the southlanders must be destroyed in order to make the lesson clear. Melniboné was still strong. She was strong enough, in Yyrkoon's view, to resume her former dominance of the world—strong in sorcery if not in soldiery.

'Hist!' Admiral Magum Colim craned forward. 'Was that the sound of an oar?'

Elric nodded. 'I think so.'

Now they heard regular splashes, as of rows of oars dipping in and out of the water, and they heard the creak of timbers. The southlanders were com-

ing. *The Son of the Pyaray* was the ship nearest to
the entrance and it would be the first to move out,
but only when the last of the southlanders' ships had
passed them. Admiral Magum Colim bent and extinguished the lantern, then, quickly, quietly, he descended to inform his crew of the raiders' coming.

Not long before, Yyrkoon had used his sorcery to
summon a peculiar mist, which hid the golden
barges from view, but through which those on the
Melnibonéan ships could peer. Now Elric saw
torches burning in the channel ahead as carefully the
reavers negotiated the maze. Within the space of a
few minutes ten of the galleys had passed the grotto.
Admiral Magum Colim rejoined Elric on the bridge
and now Prince Yyrkoon was with him. Yyrkoon,
too, wore a dragon helm, though less magnificent
than Elric's, for Elric was chief of the few surviving
Dragon Princes of Melniboné. Yyrkoon was grinning through the gloom and his eyes gleamed in anticipation of the bloodletting to come. Elric wished
that Prince Yyrkoon had chosen another ship than
this, but it was Yyrkoon's right to be aboard the
flagship and he could not deny it.

Now half the hundred vessels had gone past.

Yyrkoon's armour creaked as, impatiently, he
waited, pacing the bridge, his gauntletted hand on
the hilt of his broadsword. 'Soon' he kept saying to
himself. 'Soon.'

And then their anchor was groaning upwards and
their oars were plunging into the water as the last
southland ship went by and they shot from the
grotto into the channel ramming the enemy galley
amidships and smashing it in two.

A great yell went up from the barbarian crew.
Men were flung in all directions. Torches danced erratically on the remains of the deck as men tried to
save themselves from slipping into the dark, chill
waters of the channel. A few brave spears rattled

against the sides of the Melnibonéan flag-galley as it began to turn amongst the debris it had created. But Imrryrian archers returned the shots and the few survivors went down.

The sound of this swift conflict was the signal to the other battle-barges. In perfect order they came from both sides of the high rock walls and it must have seemed to the astonished barbarians that the great golden ships had actually emerged from solid stone—ghost ships filled with demons who rained spears, arrows and brands upon them. Now the whole of the twisting channel was confusion and a medley of war-shouts echoed and boomed and the clash of steel upon steel was like the savage hissing of some monstrous snake, and the raiding fleet itself resembled a snake which had been broken into a hundred pieces by the tall, implacable golden ships of Melniboné. These ships seemed almost serene as they moved against their enemies, their grappling irons flashing out to catch wooden decks and rails and draw the galleys nearer so that they might be destroyed.

But the southlanders were brave and they kept their heads after their initial astonishment. Three of their galleys headed directly for *The Son of the Pyaray,* recognising it as the flagship. Fire arrows sailed high and dropped down into the decks which were wooden and not protected by the golden armour, starting fires wherever they fell, or else bringing blazing death to the men they struck.

Elric raised his shield above his head and two arrows struck it, bouncing, still flaring, to a lower deck. He leapt over the rail, following the arrows, jumping down to the widest and most exposed deck where his warriors were grouping, ready to deal with the attacking galleys. Catapults thudded and balls of blue fire swished through the blackness, narrowly missing all three galleys. Another volley followed

and one mass of flame struck the far galley's mast
and then burst upon the deck, scattering huge
flames wherever it touched. Grapples snaked out
and seized the first galley, dragging it close and Elric
was amongst the first to leap down onto the deck,
rushing forward to where he saw the southland captain, dressed all in crude, chequered armour, a chequered surcoat over that, a big sword in both his
huge hands, bellowing at his men to resist the Melnibonéan dogs.

As Elric approached the bridge three barbarians
armed with curved swords and small, oblong shields
ran at him. Their faces were full of fear, but there
was determination there as well, as if they knew they
must die but planned to wreak as much destruction
as they could before their souls were taken.

Shifting his war-board onto his arm, Elric took
his own broadsword in both hands and charged the
sailors, knocking one off his feet with the lip of the
shield and smashing the collar-bone of another. The
remaining barbarian skipped aside and thrust his
curved sword at Elric's face. Elric barely escaped the
thrust and the sharp edge of the sword grazed his
cheek, bringing out a drop or two of blood. Elric
swung the broadsword like a scythe and it bit deep
into the barbarian's waist, almost cutting him in
two. He struggled for a moment, unable to believe
that he was dead but then, as Elric yanked the sword
free, he closed his eyes and dropped. The man who
had been struck by Elric's shield was staggering to
his feet as Elric whirled, saw him, and smashed the
broadsword into his skull. Now the way was clear to
the bridge. Elric began to climb the ladder, noting
that the captain had seen him and was waiting for
him at the top.

Elric raised his shield to take the captain's first
blow. Through all the noise he thought he heard the
man shouting at him.

'Die, you white-faced demon! Die! You have no place in this earth any longer!'

Elric was almost diverted from defending himself by these words. They rang true to him. Perhaps he really had no place on the earth. Perhaps that was why Melniboné was slowly collapsing, why fewer children were born every year, why the dragons themselves were no longer breeding. He let the captain strike another blow at the shield, then he reached under it and swung at the man's legs. But the captain had anticipated the move and jumped backwards. This, however, gave Elric time to run up the few remaining steps and stand on the deck, facing the captain.

The man's face was almost as pale as Elric's. He was sweating and he was panting and his eyes had misery in them as well as a wild fear.

'You should leave us alone,' Elric heard himself saying. 'We offer you no harm, barbarian. When did Melniboné last sail against the Young Kingdoms?'

'You offer us harm by your very presence, White-face. There is your sorcery. There are your customs. And there is your arrogance.'

'Is that why you came here? Was your attack motivated by disgust for us? Or would you help yourselves to our wealth? Admit it, captain—greed brought you to Melniboné.'

'At least greed is an honest quality, an understandable one. But you creatures are not human. Worse—you are not gods, though you behave as if you were. Your day is over and you must be wiped out, your city destroyed, your sorceries forgotten.'

Elric nodded. 'Perhaps you are right, captain.'

'I am right. Our holy men say so. Our seers predict your downfall. The Chaos Lords whom you serve will themselves bring about that downfall.'

'The Chaos Lords no longer have any interest in

the affairs of Melniboné. They took away their power nearly a thousand years since.' Elric watched the captain carefully, judging the distance between them. 'Perhaps that is why our own power waned. Or perhaps we merely became tired of power.'

'Be that as it may,' the captain said, wiping his sweating brow, 'your time is over. You must be destroyed once and for all.' And then he groaned, for Elric's broadsword had come under his chequered breastplate and gone up through his stomach and into his lungs.

One knee bent, one leg stretched behind him, Elric began to withdraw the long sword, looking up into the barbarian's face which had now assumed an expression of reconciliation. 'That was unfair, Whiteface. We had barely begun to talk and you cut the conversation short. You are most skillful. May you writhe forever in the Higher Hell. Farewell.'

Elric hardly knew why, after the captain had fallen face down on the deck, he hacked twice at the neck until the head rolled off the body, rolled to the side of the bridge and was then kicked over the side so that it sank into the cold, deep water.

And then Yyrkoon came up behind Elric and he was still grinning.

'You fight fiercely and well, my lord emperor. That dead man was right.'

'Right?' Elric glared at his cousin. 'Right?'

'Aye—in his assessment of your prowess.' And, chuckling, Yyrkoon went to supervise his men who were finishing off the few remaining raiders.

Elric did not know why he had refused to hate Yyrkoon before. But now he did hate Yyrkoon. At that moment he would gladly have slain him. It was as if Yyrkoon had looked deeply into Elric's soul and expressed contempt for what he had seen there.

Suddenly Elric was overwhelmed by an angry misery and he wished with all his heart that he was

not a Melnibonéan, that he was not an emperor and
that Yyrkoon had never been born.

6

Pursuit: A Deliberate Treachery

LIKE HAUGHTY Leviathans the great golden battle-barges swam through the wreckage of the reaver fleet. A few ships burned and a few were still sinking, but most had sunk into the unplumbable depths of the channel. The burning ships sent strange shadows dancing against the dank walls of the sea-caverns, as if the ghosts of the slain offered a last salute before departing to the sea-depths where, it was said, a Chaos king still ruled, crewing his eerie fleets with the souls of all who died in conflict upon the oceans of the world. Or perhaps they went to a gentler doom, serving Straasha, Lord of the Water Elementals, who ruled the upper reaches of the sea.

But a few had escaped. Somehow the southland sailors had got past the massive battle-barges, sailed back through the channel and must even now have reached the open sea. This was reported to the flagship where Elric, Magum Colim and Prince Yyrkoon now stood together again on the bridge, surveying the destruction they had wreaked.

'Then we must pursue them and finish them,' said Yyrkoon. He was sweating and his dark face glis-

tened; his eyes were alight with fever. 'We must follow them.'

Elric shrugged. He was weak. He had brought no
extra drugs with him to replenish his strength. He
wished to go back to Imrryr and rest. He was tired
of bloodletting, tired of Yyrkoon and tired, most of
all, of himself. The hatred he felt for his cousin was
draining him still further—and he hated the hatred;
that was the worst part. 'No,' he said. 'Let them go.'

'Let them go? Unpunished? Come now, my lord
king! That is not our way!' Prince Yyrkoon turned
to the aging admiral. 'Is that our way, Admiral Magum Colim?'

Magum Colim shrugged. He, too, was tired, but
privately he agreed with Prince Yyrkoon. An enemy
of Melniboné should be punished for daring even to
think of attacking the Dreaming City. Yet he said:
'The emperor must decide.'

'Let them go,' said Elric again. He leant heavily
against the rail. 'Let them carry the news back to
their own barbarian land. Let them say how the
Dragon Princes defeated them. The news will
spread. I believe we shall not be troubled by raiders
again for some time.'

'The Young Kingdoms are full of fools,' Yyrkoon
replied. 'They will not believe the news. There will
always be raiders. The best way to warn them will be
to make sure that not one southlander remains alive
or uncaptured.'

Elric drew a deep breath and tried to fight the
faintness which threatened to overwhelm him.
'Prince Yyrkoon, you are trying my patience . . .'

'But, my emperor, I think only of the good of
Melniboné. Surely you do not want your people to
say that you are weak, that you fear a fight with but
five southland galleys?'

This time Elric's anger brought him strength.
'Who will say that Elric is weak? Will it be you,

Yrkoon?' He knew that his next statement was senseless, but there was nothing he could do to stop it. 'Very well, let us pursue these poor little boats and sink them. And let us make haste. I am weary of it all.'

There was a mysterious light in Yyrkoon's eyes as he turned away to relay the orders.

The sky was turning from black to grey when the Melnibonéan fleet reached the open sea and turned its prows south towards the Boiling Sea and the southern continent beyond. The barbarian ships would not sail through the Boiling Sea—no mortal ship could do that, it was said—but would sail around it. Not that the barbarian ships would even reach the edges of the Boiling Sea, for the huge battle-barges were fast-sailing vessels. The slaves who pulled the oars were full of a drug which increased their speed and their strength for a score or so of hours, before it slew them. And now the sails billowed out, catching the breeze. Golden mountains, skimming rapidly over the sea, these ships; their method of construction was a secret lost even to the Melnibonéans (who had forgotten so much of their lore). It was easy to imagine how men of the Young Kingdoms hated Melniboné and its inventions, for it did seem that the battle-barges belonged to an older, alien age, as they bore down upon the fleeing galleys now sighted on the horizon.

The Son of the Pyaray was in the lead of the rest of the fleet and was priming its catapults well before any of its fellows had seen the enemy. Perspiring slaves gingerly manhandled the viscous stuff of the fireballs, getting them into the bronze cups of the catapults by means of long, spoon-ended tongs. It flickered in the pre-dawn gloom.

Now slaves climbed the steps to the bridge and brought wine and food on platinum platters for the

three Dragon Princes who had remained there since
the pursuit had begun. Elric could not summon the
strength to eat, but he seized a tall cup of yellow
wine and drained it. The stuff was strong and revived him a trifle. He had another cup poured and
drank that as swiftly as the other. He peered ahead.
It was almost dawn. There was a line of purple light
on the horizon. 'At the first sign of the sun's disc,'
Elric said, 'let loose the fireballs.'

'I will give the order,' said Magum Colim, wiping
his lips and putting down the meat bone on which he
had been chewing. He left the bridge. Elric heard his
feet striking the steps heavily. All at once the albino
felt surrounded by enemies. There had been something strange in Magum Colim's manner during the
argument with Prince Yyrkoon. Elric tried to shake
off such foolish thoughts. But the weariness, the
self-doubt, the open mockery of his cousin, all suc-
ceeded in increasing the feeling that he was alone
and without friends in the world. Even Cymoril and
Dyvim Tvar were, finally, Melnibonéans and could
not understand the peculiar concerns which moved
him and dictated his actions. Perhaps it would be
wise to renounce everything Melnibonéan and wan-
der the world as an anonymous soldier of fortune,
serving whoever needed his aid?

The dull red semicircle of the sun showed above
the black line of the distant water. There came a se-
ries of booming sounds from the forward decks of
the flagship as the catapults released their fiery shot;
there was a whistling scream, fading away, and it
seemed that a dozen meteors leapt through the sky,
hurtling towards the five galleys which were now little more than thirty ship-lengths away.

Elric saw two galleys flare, but the remaining
three began to sail a zig-zag course and avoided the
fireballs which landed on the water and burned fit-

fully for a while before sinking (still burning) into
the depths.

More fireballs were prepared and Elric heard
Yyrkoon shout from the other side of the bridge, ordering the slaves to greater exertions. Then the fleeing vessels changed their tactics, evidently realising
that they could not save themselves for long, and,
spreading out, sailed towards *The Son of the Pyaray,* just as the other ships had done in the sea-
maze. It was not merely their courage that Elric
admired but their manoeuvring skill and the speed
at which they had arrived at this logical, if hopeless,
decision.

The sun was behind the southland ships as they
turned. Three brave silhouettes drew nearer to the
Melnibonéan flagship as scarlet stained the sea, as if
in anticipation of the bloodletting to come.

Another volley of fireballs was flung from the
flagship and the leading galley tried to tack round
and avoid it, but two of the fiery globes spattered directly on its deck and soon the whole ship was alive
with flame. Burning men leapt into the water. Burning men shot arrows at the flagship. Burning men
fell slowly from their positions in the rigging. The
burning men died, but the burning ship came on;
someone had lashed the steering arm and directed
the galley at *The Son of the Pyaray.* It crashed into
the golden side of the battle-barge and some of the
fire splashed on the deck where the main catapults
were in position. A cauldron containing the fire-
stuff caught and immediately men were running
from all quarters of the ship to try to douse the
flame. Elric grinned as he saw what the barbarians
had done. Perhaps that ship had deliberately allowed itself to be fired. Now the majority of the
flagship's complement was engaged with putting out
the blaze—while the southland ships drew along-

side, threw up their own grapples, and began to board.

' 'Ware boarders!' Elric shouted, long after he might have warned his crew. 'Barbarians attack.'

He saw Yyrkoon whirl round, see the situation, and rush down the steps from the bridge. 'You stay there, my lord king,' he flung at Elric as he disappeared. 'You are plainly too weary to fight.'

And Elric summoned all that was left of his strength and stumbled after his cousin, to help in the defense of the ship.

The barbarians were not fighting for their lives— they knew those to be taken already. They were fighting for their pride. They wanted to take one Melnibonéan ship down with them and that ship must be the flagship itself. It was hard to be contemptuous of such men. They knew that even if they took the flagship the other ships of the golden fleet would soon overwhelm them.

But the other ships were still some distance away. Many lives would be lost before they reached the flagship.

On the lowest deck Elric found himself facing a pair of tall barbarians, each armed with a curved blade and a small, oblong shield. He lunged forward, but his armour seemed to drag at his limbs, his own shield and sword were so heavy that he could barely lift them. Two swords struck his helm, almost simultaneously. He lunged back and caught a man in the arm, rammed the other with his shield. A curved blade clanged on his backplate and he all but lost his footing. There was choking smoke everywhere, and heat, and the tumult of battle. Desperately he swung about him and felt his broadsword bite deep into flesh. One of his opponents fell, gurgling, with blood spouting from his mouth and nose. The other lunged. Elric stepped backwards, fell over the corpse of the man he had slain, and went down, his broadsword held out before him in one hand. And as the triumphant barbarian leapt forward to finish the albino, Elric caught him on the point of the broadsword, running him through. The dead man fell towards Elric who did not feel the impact, for he had already fainted. Not for the first time had his deficient blood, no longer enriched by drugs, betrayed him.

He tasted salt and thought at first it was blood. But it was sea water. A wave had risen over the deck and momentarily revived him. He struggled to crawl from under the dead man and then he heard a voice he recognised. He twisted his head and looked up.

Prince Yyrkoon stood there. He was grinning. He was full of glee at Elric's plight. Black, oily smoke still drifted everywhere, but the sounds of the fight had died.

'Are—are we victorious, cousin?' Elric spoke painfully.

'Aye. The barbarians are all dead now. We are about to sail for Imrryr.'

Elric was relieved. He would begin to die soon if he could not get to his store of potions.

His relief must have been evident, for Yyrkoon laughed. 'It is as well the battle did not last longer, my lord, or we should have been without our leader.'

'Help me up, cousin.' Elric hated to ask Prince Yyrkoon any favour, but he had no choice. He stretched out his empty hand. 'I am fit enough to inspect the ship.'

Yyrkoon came forward as if to take the hand, but then he hesitated, still grinning. 'But, my lord, I disagree. You will be dead by the time this ship turns eastward again.'

'Nonsense. Even without the drugs I can live for a considerable time, though movement is difficult. Help me up, Yyrkoon, I command you.'

'You cannot command me, Elric. I am emperor now, you see.'

'Be wary, cousin. I can overlook such treachery, but others will not. I shall be forced to . . .'

Yyrkoon swung his legs over Elric's body and went to the rail. Here were bolts which fixed one section of the rail in place when it was not used for the gangplank. Yyrkoon slowly released the bolts and kicked the section of rail into the water.

Now Elric's efforts to free himself became more desperate. But he could hardly move at all.

Yyrkoon, on the other hand, seemed possessed of unnatural strength. He bent and easily flung the corpse away from Elric.

'Yyrkoon,' said Elric, 'this is unwise of you.'

'I was never a cautious man, cousin, as well as you know.' Yyrkoon placed a booted foot against Elric's ribs and began to shove. Elric slid towards the gap in the rail. He could see the black sea heaving below. 'Farewell, Elric. Now a true Melnibonéan shall sit upon the Ruby Throne. And, who knows, might even make Cymoril his queen? It has not been unheard of . . .'

And Elric felt himself rolling, felt himself fall, felt himself strike the water, felt his armour pulling him below the surface. And Yyrkoon's last words drummed in Elric's ears like the persistent booming of the waves against the sides of the golden battle-barge.

BOOK TWO

Less certain of himself or his destiny than ever, the albino king must perforce bring his powers of sorcery into play, conscious that he has embarked upon a course of action by no means at one with his original conception of the way he wished to live his life. And now matters must be settled. He must begin to rule. He must become cruel. But even in this he will find himself thwarted.

BOOK TWO

1

The Caverns of the Sea King

ELRIC SANK RAPIDLY, desperately trying to keep the last of his breath in his body. He had no strength to swim and the weight of the armour denied any hope of his rising to the surface and being sighted by Magum Colim or one of the others still loyal to him.

The roaring in his ears gradually faded to a whisper so that it sounded as if little voices were speaking to him, the voices of the water elementals with whom, in his youth, he had had a kind of friendship. And the pain in his lungs faded; the red mist cleared from his eyes and he thought he saw the face of his father, Sadric, of Cymoril and, fleetingly, of Yyrkoon. Stupid Yyrkoon: for all that he prided himself that he was a Melnibonéan, he lacked the Melnibonéan subtlety. He was as brutal and direct as some of the Young Kingdom barbarians he so much despised. And now Elric began to feel almost grateful to his cousin. His life was over. The conflicts which tore his mind would no longer trouble him. His fears, his torments, his loves and his hatreds all lay in the past and only oblivion lay before him. As the last of his breath left his body, he gave himself

wholly to the sea; to Straasha, Lord of all the Water
Elementals, once the comrade of the Melnibonéan
folk. And as he did this he remembered the old spell
which his ancestors had used to summon Straasha.
The spell came unbidden into his dying brain.

> *Waters of the sea, thou gave us birth*
> *And were our milk and mother both*
> *In days when skies were overcast*
> *You who were first shall be the last.*

> *Sea-rulers, fathers of our blood,*
> *Thine aid is sought, thine aid is sought,*
> *Your salt is blood, our blood your salt,*
> *Your blood the blood of Man.*

> *Straasha, eternal king, eternal sea*
> *Thine aid is sought by me;*
> *For enemies of thine and mine*
> *Seek to defeat our destiny, and drain*
> *away our sea.*

Either the words had an old, symbolic meaning or
they referred to some incident in Melnibonéan history which even Elric had not read about. The
words meant very little to him and yet they continued to repeat themselves as his body sank deeper
and deeper into the green waters. Even when blackness overwhelmed him and his lungs filled with
water, the words continued to whisper through the
corridors of his brain. It was strange that he should
be dead and still hear the incantation.

It seemed a long while later that his eyes opened and
revealed swirling water and, through it, huge, indis-
tinct figures gliding towards him. Death, it appeared, took a long time to come and, while he died,

he dreamed. The leading figure had a turquoise
beard and hair, pale green skin that seemed made of
the sea itself and, when he spoke, a voice that was
like a rushing tide. He smiled at Elric.

*Straasha answers thy summons, mortal. Our des-
tinies are bound together. How may I aid thee, and,
in aiding thee, aid myself?*

Elric's mouth was filled with water and yet he
still seemed capable of speech (thus proving he
dreamed).

He said:

'King Straasha. The paintings in the Tower of
D'a'rputna—in the library. When I was a boy I saw
them, King Straasha.'

The sea-king stretched out his sea-green hands.
*'Aye. You sent the summons. You need our aid. We
honour our ancient pact with your folk.'*

'No. I did not mean to summon you. The summons came unbidden to my dying mind. I am happy
to drown, King Straasha.'

*'That cannot be. If your mind summoned us it
means you wish to live. We will aid you.'* King
Straasha's beard streamed in the tide and his deep,
green eyes were gentle, almost tender, as they regarded the albino.

Elric closed his own eyes again. 'I dream,' he said.
'I deceive myself with fantasies of hope.' He felt
the water in his lungs and he knew he no longer
breathed. It stood to reason, therefore, that he was
dead. 'But if you were real, old friend, and you
wished to aid me, you would return me to Melniboné so that I might deal with the usurper, Yyrkoon,
and save Cymoril, before it is too late. That is my
only regret—the torment which Cymoril will suffer
if her brother becomes Emperor of Melniboné.'

'Is that all you ask of the water elementals?' King
Straasha seemed almost disappointed.

'I do not even ask that of you. I only voice what I

would have wished, had this been reality and I was speaking, which I know is impossible. Now I shall die.'

'That cannot be, Lord Elric, for our destinies are truly intertwined and I know that it is not yet your destiny to perish. Therefore I will aid you as you have suggested.'

Elric was surprised at the sharpness of detail of this fantasy. He said to himself. 'What a cruel torment I subject myself to. Now I must set about admitting my death . . .'

'You cannot die. Not yet.'

Now it was as if the sea-king's gentle hands had picked him up and bore him through twisting corridors of a delicate coral pink texture, slightly shadowed, no longer in water. And Elric felt the water vanish from his lungs and stomach and he breathed. Could it be that he had actually been brought to the legendary plane of the elemental folk—a plane which intersected that of the earth and in which they dwelled, for the most part?

In a huge, circular cavern, which shone with pink and blue mother-of-pearl, they came to rest at last. The sea-king laid Elric down upon the floor of the cavern, which seemed to be covered with fine, white sand which was yet not sand for it yielded and then sprang back when he moved.

When King Straasha moved, it was with a sound like the tide drawing itself back over shingle. The sea-king crossed the white sand, walking towards a large throne of milky jade. He seated himself upon this throne and placed his green head on his green fist, regarding Elric with puzzled, yet compassionate, eyes.

Elric was still physically weak, but he could breathe. It was as if the sea water had filled him and then cleansed him when it was driven out. He felt clear-headed. And now he was much less sure that he dreamed.

'I still find it hard to know why you saved me, King Straasha,' he murmured from where he lay on the sand.

'The rune. We heard it on this plane and we came. That is all.'

'Aye. But there is more to sorcery-working than that. There are chants, symbols, rituals of all sorts. Previously that has always been true.'

'Perhaps the rituals take the place of urgent need of the kind which sent out your summons to us. Though you say you wished to die, it was evident you did not really want to die or the summoning would not have been so clear and have reached us so swiftly. Forget all this now. When you have rested, we shall do what you have requested of us.'

Painfully, Elric raised himself into a sitting position. 'You spoke earlier of "intertwined destinies". Do you, then, know something of my destiny?'

'A little, I think. Our world grows old. Once the elementals were powerful on your plane and the people of Melniboné all shared that power. But now our power wanes, as does yours. Something is changing. There are intimations that the Lords of the Higher Worlds are again taking an interest in your world. Perhaps they fear that the folk of the Young Kingdoms have forgotten them. Perhaps the folk of the Young Kingdoms threaten to bring in a new age, where gods and beings such as myself no longer shall have a place. I suspect there is a certain unease upon the planes of the Higher Worlds.'

'You know no more?'

King Straasha raised his head and looked directly into Elric's eyes. *'There is no more I can tell you, son of my old friends, save that you would be happier if you gave yourself up entirely to your destiny when you understand it.'*

Elric sighed. 'I think I know of what you speak,

King Straasha. I shall try to follow your advice.'

'And now that you have rested, it is time to return.'

The sea-king rose from his throne of milky jade and flowed towards Elric, lifting him up in strong, green arms.

'We shall meet again before your life ends, Elric. I hope that I shall be able to aid you once more. And remember that our brothers of the air and of fire will try to aid you also. And remember the beasts—they, too, can be of service to you. There is no need to suspect their help. But beware of gods, Elric. Beware of the Lords of the Higher Worlds and remember that their aid and their gifts must always be paid for.'

These were the last words Elric heard the sea-king speak before they rushed again through the sinuous tunnels of this other plane, moving at such a speed that Elric could distinguish no details and, at times, did not know whether they remained in King Straasha's kingdom or had returned to the depths of his own world's sea.

2

A New Emperor and an Emperor Renewed

STRANGE CLOUDS FILLED the sky and the sun hung heavy and huge and red behind them and the ocean was black as the golden galleys swept homeward before their battered flagship *The Son of the Pyaray* which moved slowly with dead slaves at her oars and her tattered sails limp at their masts and smoke-begrimed men on her decks and a new emperor upon her war-wrecked bridge. The new emperor was the only jubilant man in the fleet and he was jubilant indeed. It was his banner now, not Elric's, which took pride of place on the flagmast, for he had lost no time in proclaiming Elric slain and himself ruler of Melniboné.

To Yyrkoon, the peculiar sky was an omen of change, of a return to the old ways and the old power of the Dragon Isle. When he issued orders, his voice was a veritable croon of pleasure, and Admiral Magum Colim, who had ever been wary of Elric but who now had to obey Yyrkoon's orders, wondered if, perhaps, it would not have been preferable to have dealt with Yyrkoon in the manner in which (he suspected) Yyrkoon had dealt with Elric.

Dyvim Tvar leaned on the rail of his own ship, *Terhali's Particular Satisfaction,* and he also paid attention to the sky, though he saw omens of doom, for he mourned for Elric and considered how he might take vengeance on Prince Yyrkoon, should it emerge that Yyrkoon had murdered his cousin for possession of the Ruby Throne.

Melniboné appeared on the horizon, a brooding silhouette of crags, a dark monster squatting in the sea, calling her own back to the heated pleasures of her womb, the Dreaming City of Imrryr. The great cliffs loomed, the central gate to the sea-maze opened, water slapped and gasped as the golden prows disturbed it and the golden ships were swallowed into the murky dankness of the tunnels where bits of wreckage still floated from the previous night's encounter; where white, bloated corpses could still be seen when the brandlight touch them. The prows nosed arrogantly through the remains of their prey, but there was no joy aboard the golden battle-barges, for they brought news of their old emperor's death in battle (Yyrkoon had told them what had happened). Next night and for seven nights in all the Wild Dance of Melniboné would fill the streets. Potions and petty spells would ensure that no-one slept, for sleep was forbidden to any Melnibonéan, old or young, while a dead emperor was mourned. Naked, the Dragon Princes would prowl the city, taking any young woman they found and filling her with their seed for it was traditional that if an emperor died then the nobles of Melniboné must create as many children of aristocratic blood as was possible. Music-slaves would howl from the top of every tower. Other slaves would be slain and some eaten. It was a dreadful dance, the Dance of Misery, and it took as many lives as it created. A tower would be pulled down and a new one erected during those seven days and the tower would be called for Elric VIII, the Albino Emperor, slain upon the sea, defending Melniboné against the southland pirates.

Slain upon the sea and his body taken by the waves. That was not a good portent, for it meant that Elric had gone to serve Pyaray, the Tentacled Whisperer of Impossible Secrets, the Chaos Lord who commanded the Chaos Fleet—dead ships, dead sailors, forever in his thrall—and it was not fitting that such a fate should befall one of the Royal Line of Melniboné. Ah, but the mourning would be long, thought Dyvim Tvar. He had loved Elric, for all that he had sometimes disapproved of his methods of ruling the Dragon Isle. Secretly he would go to the Dragon Caves that night and spend the period of mourning with the sleeping dragons who, now that Elric was dead, were all he had left to love. And Dyvim Tvar then thought of Cymoril, awaiting Elric's return.

The ships began to emerge into the half-light of the evening. Torches and braziers already burned on the quays of Imrryr which were deserted save for a small group of figures who stood around a chariot which had been driven out to the end of the central mole. A cold wind blew. Dyvim Tvar knew that it was the Princess Cymoril who waited, with her guards, for the fleet.

Though the flagship was the last to pass through the maze, the rest of the ships had to wait until it could be towed into position and dock first. If this had not been the required tradition, Dyvim Tvar would have left his ship and gone to speak to Cymoril, escort her from the quay and tell her what he knew of the circumstances of Elric's death. But it was impossible. Even before *Terhali's Particular Satisfaction* had dropped anchor, the main gangplank of *The Son of the Pyaray* had been lowered and the Emperor Yyrkoon, all swaggering pride, had stepped down it, his arms raised in triumphant salute to his sister who could be seen, even now, searching the decks of the ships for a sign of her beloved albino.

Suddenly Cymoril knew that Elric was dead and she suspected that Yyrkoon had, in some way, been responsible for Elric's death. Either Yyrkoon had allowed Elric to be borne down by a group of southland reavers or else he had managed to slay Elric himself. She knew her brother and she recognised his expression. He was pleased with himself as he always had been when successful in some form of treachery or another. Anger flashed in her tear-filled eyes and she threw back her head and shouted at the shifting, ominous sky:

'Oh! Yyrkoon has destroyed him!'

Her guards were startled. The captain spoke solicitously. 'Madam?'

'He is dead—and that brother slew him. Take Prince Yyrkoon, captain. Kill Prince Yyrkoon, captain.'

Unhappily, the captain put his right hand on the hilt of his sword. A young warrior, more impetuous, drew his blade, murmuring: 'I will slay him, princess, if that is your desire.' The young warrior loved Cymoril with considerable and unthinking intensity.

The captain offered the warrior a cautionary glance, but the warrior was blind to it. Now two others slid swords from scabbards as Yyrkoon, a red cloak wound about him, his dragon crest catching the light from the brands guttering in the wind, stalked forward and cried:

'Yyrkoon is emperor now!'

'No!' shrieked Yyrkoon's sister. 'Elric! Elric! Where are you?'

'Serving his new master, Pyaray of Chaos. His dead hands pull at the sweep of a Chaos ship, sister. His dead eyes see nothing at all. His dead ears hear only the crack of Pyaray's whips and his dead flesh cringes, feeling nought but that unearthly scourge. Elric sank in his armour to the bottom of the sea.'

'Murderer! Traitor!' Cymoril began to sob.

The captain, who was a practical man, said to his warriors in a low voice: 'Sheath your weapons and salute your new emperor.'

Only the young guardsman who loved Cymoril disobeyed. 'But he slew the emperor! My lady Cymoril said so!'

'What of it? He is emperor now. Kneel or you'll be dead within the minute.'

The young warrior gave a wild shout and leapt towards Yyrkoon, who stepped back, trying to free his arms from the folds of his cloak. He had not expected this.

But it was the captain who leapt forward, his own sword drawn, and hacked down the youngster so that he gasped, half-turned, then fell at Yyrkoon's feet.

This demonstration of the captain's was confirmation of his real power and Yyrkoon almost smirked with satisfaction as he looked down at the corpse. The captain fell to one knee, the bloody sword still in his hand. 'My emperor,' he said.

'You show a proper loyalty, captain.'

'My loyalty is to the Ruby Throne.'

'Quite so.'

Cymoril shook with grief and rage, but her rage was impotent. She knew now that she had no friends.

Leering, the Emperor Yyrkoon presented himself before her. He reached out his hand and he caressed her neck, her cheek, her mouth. He let his hand fall so that it grazed her breast. 'Sister,' he said, 'thou art mine entirely now.'

And Cymoril was the second to fall at his feet, for she had fainted.

'Pick her up,' Yyrkoon said to the guard. 'Take
her back to her own tower and there be sure she remains. Two guards will be with her at all times, in
even her most private moments they must observe
her, for she may plan treachery against the Ruby
Throne.'

The captain bowed and signed to his men to obey
the emperor. 'Aye, my lord. It shall be done.'

Yyrkoon looked back at the corpse of the young
warrior. 'And feed that to her slaves tonight, so that
he can continue serving her.' He smiled.

The captain smiled, too, appreciating the joke.
He felt it was good to have a proper emperor in Melniboné again. An emperor who knew how to behave, who knew how to treat his enemies and who
accepted unswerving loyalty as his right. The captain fancied that fine, martial times lay ahead for
Melniboné. The golden battle-barges and the warriors of Imrryr could go a-spoiling again and instil in
the barbarians of the Young Kingdoms a sweet and
satisfactory sense of fear. Already, in his mind, the
captain helped himself to the treasures of Lormyr,
Argimiliar and Pikarayd, of Ilmiora and Jadmar.
He might even be made governor, say, of the Isle of
the Purple Towns. What luxuries of torment would
he bring to those upstart sealords, particularly
Count Smiorgan Baldhead who was even now beginning to try to make the isle a rival to Melniboné
as a trading port. As he escorted the limp body of
the Princess Cymoril back to her tower, the captain
looked on that body and felt the swellings of lust
within him. Yyrkoon would reward his loyalty, there
was no doubt of that. Despite the cold wind, the
captain began to sweat in his anticipation. He, himself, would guard the Princess Cymoril. He would
relish it.

Marching at the head of his army, Yyrkoon strutted

for the Tower of D'arputna, the Tower of Emperors, and the Ruby Throne within. He preferred to ignore the litter which had been brought for him and to go on foot, so that he might savour every small moment of his triumph. He approached the tower, tall among its fellows at the very centre of Imrryr, as he might approach a beloved woman. He approached it with a sense of delicacy and without haste, for he knew that it was his.

He looked about him. His army marched behind him. Magum Colim and Dyvim Tvar led the army. People lined the twisting streets and bowed low to him. Slaves prostrated themselves. Even the beasts of burden were made to kneel as he strode by. Yyrkoon could almost taste the power as one might taste a luscious fruit. He drew deep breaths of the air. Even the air was his. All Imrryr was his. All Melniboné. Soon would all the world be his. And he would squander it all. How he would squander it! Such a grand terror would he bring back to the earth; such a munificence of fear! In ecstasy, almost blindly, did the Emperor Yyrkoon enter the tower. He hesitated at the great doors of the throne room. He signed for the doors to be opened and as they opened he deliberately took in the scene tiny bit by tiny bit. The walls, the banners, the trophies, the galleries, all were his. The throne room was empty now, but soon he would fill it with colour and celebration and true, Melnibonéan entertainments. It had been too long since blood had sweetened the air of this hall. Now he let his eyes linger upon the steps leading up to the Ruby Throne itself, but, before he looked at the throne, he heard Dyvim Tvar gasp behind him and his gaze went suddenly to the Ruby Throne and his jaw slackened at what he saw. His eyes widened in incredulity.

'An illusion!'

'An apparition,' said Dyvim Tvar with some satisfaction.

'Heresy!' cried the Emperor Yyrkoon, staggering
forward, finger pointing at the robed and cowled
figure which sat so still upon the Ruby Throne.
'Mine! Mine!'

The figure made no reply.

'Mine! Begone! The throne belongs to Yyrkoon.
Yyrkoon is emperor now! What are you? Why
would you thwart me thus?'

The cowl fell back and a bone-white face was revealed, surrounded by flowing, milk-white hair.
Crimson eyes looked coolly down at the shrieking,
stumbling thing which came towards them.

'You are dead, Elric! I know that you are dead!'

The apparition made no reply, but a thin smile
touched the white lips.

'You *could* not have survived. You drowned. You
cannot come back. Pyaray owns your soul!'

'There are others who rule in the sea,' said the figure on the Ruby Throne. 'Why did you slay me,
cousin?'

Yyrkoon's guile had deserted him, making way
for terror and confusion. 'Because it is my right to
rule! Because you were not strong enough, nor cruel
enough, nor humorous enough . . .'

'Is this not a good joke, cousin?'

'Begone! Begone! Begone! I shall not be ousted
by a spectre! A dead emperor cannot rule Melniboné!'

'We shall see,' said Elric, signing to Dyvim Tvar
and his soldiers.

3

A Traditional Justice

'NOW INDEED I shall rule as you would have had me rule, cousin.' Elric watched as Dyvim Tvar's soldiers surrounded the would-be usurper and seized his arms, relieving him of his weapons.

Yyrkoon panted like a captured wolf. He glared around him as if hoping to find support from the assembled warriors, but they stared back at him either neutrally or with open contempt.

'And you, Prince Yyrkoon, will be the first to benefit from this new rule of mine. Are you pleased?'

Yyrkoon lowered his head. He was trembling now. Elric laughed. 'Speak up, cousin.'

'May Arioch and all the Dukes of Hell torment you for eternity,' growled Yyrkoon. He flung back his head, his wild eyes rolling, his lips curling: 'Arioch! Arioch! Curse this feeble albino! Arioch! Destroy him or see Melniboné fall!'

Elric continued to laugh. 'Arioch does not hear you. Chaos is weak upon the earth now. It needs a greater sorcery than yours to bring the Chaos Lords back to aid you as they aided our ancestors. And now, Yyrkoon, tell me—where is the Lady Cymoril?'

But Yyrkoon had lapsed, again, into a sullen silence.

'She is at her own tower, my emperor,' said Magum Colim.

'A creature of Yyrkoon's took her there,' said Dyvim Tvar. 'The captain of Cymoril's own guard, he slew a warrior who tried to defend his mistress against Yyrkoon. It could be that Princess Cymoril is in danger, my lord.'

'Then go quickly to the tower. Take a force of men. Bring both Cymoril and the captain of her guard to me.'

'And Yyrkoon, my lord?' asked Dyvim Tvar.

'Let him remain here until his sister returns.'

Dyvim Tvar bowed and, selecting a body of warriors, left the throne room. All noticed that Dyvim Tvar's step was lighter and his expression less grim than when he had first approached the throne room at Prince Yyrkoon's back.

Yyrkoon straightened his head and looked about the court. For a moment he seemed like a pathetic and bewildered child. All the lines of hate and anger had disappeared and Elric felt sympathy for his cousin growing again within him. But this time Elric quelled the feeling.

'Be grateful, cousin, that for a few hours you were totally powerful, that you enjoyed domination over all the folk of Melniboné.'

Yyrkoon said in a small, puzzled voice: 'How did you escape? You had no time for making a sorcery, no strength for it. You could barely move your limbs and your armour must have dragged you deep to the bottom of the sea so that you should have drowned. It is unfair, Elric. You should have drowned.'

Elric shrugged, 'I have friends in the sea. They re-

cognise my royal blood and my right to rule if you
do not.'

Yyrkoon tried to disguise the astonishment he
felt. Evidently his respect for Elric had increased, as
had his hatred for the albino emperor. 'Friends.'

'Aye,' said Elric with a thin grin.

'I—I thought, too, you had vowed not to use your
powers of sorcery.'

'But you thought that a vow which was unbefit-
ting for a Melnibonéan monarch to make, did you
not? Well, I agree with you. You see, Yyrkoon, you
have won a victory, after all.'

Yyrkoon stared narrowly at Elric, as if trying to
divine a secret meaning behind Elric's words. 'You
will bring back the Chaos Lords?'

'No sorcerer, however powerful, can summon the
Chaos Lords or, for that matter, the Lords of Law,
if they do not wish to be summoned. That you
know. You must know it, Yyrkoon. Have you not,
yourself, tried. And Arioch did not come, did he?
Did he bring you the gift you sought—the gift of the
two black swords?'

'You know that?'

'I did not. I guessed. Now I know.'

Yyrkoon tried to speak but his voice would not
form words, so angry was he. Instead, a strangled
growl escaped his throat and for a few moments he
struggled in the grip of his guards.

Dyvim Tvar returned with Cymoril. The girl was
pale but she was smiling. She ran into the throne
room. 'Elric!'

'Cymoril! Are you harmed?'

Cymoril glanced at the crestfallen captain of her
guard who had been brought with her. A look of disgust crossed her fine face. Then she shook her head.
'No. I am not harmed.'

The captain of Cymoril's guard was shaking with

terror. He looked pleadingly at Yyrkoon as if hoping that his fellow prisoner could help him. But Yyrkoon continued to stare at the floor.

'Have that one brought closer.' Elric pointed at the captain of the guard. The man was dragged to the foot of the steps leading to the Ruby Throne. He moaned. 'What a petty traitor you are,' said Elric. 'At least Yyrkoon had the courage to attempt to slay me. And his ambitions were high. Your ambition was merely to become one of his pet curs. So you betrayed your mistress and slew one of your own men. What is your name?'

The man had difficulty speaking, but at last he murmured, 'It is Valharik, my name. What could I do? I serve the Ruby Throne, whoever sits upon it.'

'So the traitor claims that loyalty motivated him. I think not.'

'It was, my lord. It was.' The captain began to whine. He fell to his knees. 'Slay me swiftly. Do not punish me more.'

Elric's impulse was to heed the man's request, but he looked at Yyrkoon and then remembered the expression on Cymoril's face when she had looked at the guard. He knew that he must make a point now, whilst making an example of Captain Valharik. So he shook his head. 'No. I will punish you more. Tonight you will die here according to the traditions of Melniboné, while my nobles feast to celebrate this new era of my rule.'

Valharik began to sob. Then he stopped himself and got slowly to his feet, a Melnibonéan again. He bowed low and stepped backward, giving himself into the grip of his guards.

'I must consider a way in which your fate may be shared with the one you wished to serve,' Elric went on. 'How did you slay the young warrior who sought to obey Cymoril?'

'With my sword. I cut him down. It was a clean

stroke. But one.'

'And what became of the corpse.'

'Prince Yyrkoon told me to feed it to Princess Cymoril's slaves.'

'I understand. Very well, Prince Yyrkoon, you may join us at the feast tonight while Captain Valharik entertains us with his dying.'

Yyrkoon's face was almost as pale as Elric's. 'What do you mean?'

'The little pieces of Captain Valharik's flesh which our Doctor Jest will carve from his limbs will be the meat on which you feast. You may give instructions as to how you wish the captain's flesh prepared. We should not expect you to eat it raw, cousin.'

Even Dyvim Tvar looked astonished at Elric's decision. Certainly it was in the spirit of Melniboné and a clever irony improving on Prince Yyrkoon's own idea, but it was unlike Elric— or, at least, it was unlike the Elric he had known up until a day earlier.

As he heard his fate, Captain Valharik gave a great scream of terror and glared at Prince Yyrkoon as if the would-be usurper were already tasting his flesh. Yyrkoon tried to turn away, his shoulders shaking.

'And that will be the beginning of it,' said Elric. 'The feast will start at midnight. Until that time, confine Yyrkoon to his own tower.'

After Prince Yyrkoon and Captain Valharik had been led away, Dyvim Tvar and Princess Cymoril came and stood beside Elric who had sunk back in his great throne and was staring bitterly into the middle-distance.

'That was a clever cruelty,' Dyvim Tvar said.

Cymoril said: 'It is what they both deserve.'

'Aye,' murmured Elric. 'It is what my father would have done. It is what Yyrkoon would have done had our positions been reversed. I but follow the traditions. I no longer pretend that I am my own man. Here I shall stay until I die, trapped upon the Ruby Throne—serving the Ruby Throne as Valharik claimed to serve it.'

'Could you not kill them both quickly?' Cymoril asked. 'You know that I do not plead for my brother because he is my brother. I hate him most of all. But it might destroy you, Elric, to follow through with your plan.'

'What if it does? Let me be destroyed. Let me merely become an unthinking extension of my ancestors. The puppet of ghosts and memories, dancing to strings which extend back through time for ten thousand years.'

'Perhaps if you slept . . .' Dyvim Tvar suggested.

'I shall not sleep, I feel, for many nights after this. But your brother is not going to die, Cymoril. After his punishment—after he has eaten the flesh of Captain Valharik—I intend to send him into exile. He will go alone into the Young Kingdoms and he will not be allowed to take his grimoires with him. He must make his way as best he can in the lands of the barbarian. That is not too severe a punishment, I think.'

'It is too lenient,' said Cymoril. 'You would be best advised to slay him. Send soldiers now. Give him no time to consider counterplots.'

'I do not fear his counterplots.' Elric rose wearily. 'Now I should like it if you would both leave me, until an hour or so before the feasting begins. I must think.'

'I will return to my tower and prepare myself for tonight,' said Cymoril. She kissed Elric lightly upon his pale forehead. He looked up, filled with love and tenderness for her. He reached out and touched her hair and her cheek. 'Remember that I love you, Elric,' she said.

'I will see that you are safely escorted homeward,' Dyvim Tvar said to her. 'And you must choose a new commander of your guard. Can I assist in that?'

'I should be grateful, Dyvim Tvar.'

They left Elric still upon the Ruby Throne, still staring into space. The hand that he lifted from time to time to his pale head shook a little and now the torment showed in his strange, crimson eyes.

Later, he rose up from the Ruby Throne and walked slowly, head bowed, to his own apartments, followed by his guards. He hesitated at the door which led onto the steps going up to the library. Instinctively he sought the consolation and forgetfulness of a certain kind of knowledge, but at that moment he suddenly hated his scrolls and his books. He blamed them for his ridiculous concerns regarding 'morality' and 'justice'; he blamed them for the feelings of guilt and despair which now filled him as a result of his decision to behave as a Melnibonéan monarch was expected to behave. So he passed the door to the library and went on to his apartments, but even his apartments displeased him now. They were austere. They were not furnished according to the luxurious tastes of all Melnibonéans (save for his father) with their delight in lush mixtures of colour and bizarre design. He would have them changed as soon as possible. He would give himself up to those ghosts who ruled him. For some time he stalked from room to room, trying to push back that part of him which demanded he be merciful to Valharik and to Yyrkoon—at very least to slay them and be done with it or, better, to send them both into exile. But it was impossible to reverse his decision now.

At last he lowered himself to a couch which rested beside a window looking out over the whole of the city. The sky was still full of turbulent cloud, but now the moon shone through, like the yellow eye of an unhealthy beast. It seemed to stare with a certain triumphant irony at him, as if relishing the defeat of his conscience. Elric sank his head into his arms.

Later the servants came to tell him that the courtiers were assembling for the celebration feast. He allowed them to dress him in his yellow robes of state and to place the dragon crown upon his head and then he returned to the throne room to be greeted by a mighty cheer, more wholehearted than any he had ever received before. He acknowledged the greeting and then seated himself in the Ruby Throne, looking out over the banqueting tables which now filled the hall. A table was brought and set before him and two extra seats were brought, for Dyvim Tvar and Cymoril would sit beside him. But Dyvim Tvar and Cymoril were not yet here and neither had the renegade Valharik been brought. And where was Yyrkoon? They should, even now, be at the centre of the hall—Valharik in chains and Yyrkoon seated beneath him. Doctor Jest was there, heating his brazier on which rested his cooking pans, testing and sharpening his knives. The hall was filled with excited talk as the court waited to be entertained. Already the food was being brought in, though no one might eat until the emperor ate first.

Elric signed to the commander of his own guard. 'Has the Princess Cymoril or Lord Dyvim Tvar arrived at the tower yet?'

'No, my lord.'

Cymoril was rarely late and Dyvim Tvar never. Elric frowned. Perhaps they did not relish the entertainment.

'And what of the prisoners?'

'They have been sent for, my lord.'

Doctor Jest looked up expectantly, his thin body tensed in anticipation.

And then Elric heard a sound above the din of the conversation. A groaning sound which seemed to

come from all around the tower. He bent his head
and listened closely.

Others were hearing it now. They stopped talking
and also listened intently. Soon the whole hall was in
silence and the groaning increased.

Then, all at once, the doors of the throne room
burst open and there was Dyvim Tvar, gasping and
bloody, his clothes slashed and his flesh gashed.
And following him in came a mist—a swirling mist
of dark purples and unpleasant blues and it was this
mist that groaned.

Elric sprang from his throne and knocked the table aside. He leapt down the steps towards his
friend. The groaning mist began to creep further
into the throne room, as if reaching out for Dyvim
Tvar.

Elric took his friend in his arms. 'Dyvim Tvar!
What is this sorcery?'

Dyvim Tvar's face was full of horror and his lips
seemed frozen until at last he said:

'It is Yyrkoon's sorcery. He conjured the groaning
mist to aid him in his escape. I tried to follow him
from the city but the mist engulfed me and I lost my
senses. I went to his tower to bring him and his ac-
cessory here, but the sorcery had already been ac-
complished.'

'Cymoril? Where is she?'

'He took her, Elric. She is with him. Valharik is
with him and so are a hundred warriors who remained secretly loyal to him.'

'Then we must pursue him. We shall soon capture
him.'

'You can do nothing against the groaning mist.
Ah! It comes!'

And sure enough the mist was beginning to surround them. Elric tried to disperse it by waving his
arms, but then it had gathered thickly around him
and its melancholy groaning filled his ears, its

hideous colours blinded his eyes. He tried to rush through it, but it remained with him. And now he thought he heard words amongst the groans. 'Elric is weak. Elric is foolish. Elric must die!'

'Stop this!' he cried. He bumped into another body and fell to his knees. He began to crawl, desperately trying to peer through the mist. Now faces formed in the mist—frightful faces, more terrifying than any he had ever seen, even in his worst nightmares.

'Cymoril!' he cried. 'Cymoril!'

And one of the faces became the face of Cymoril—a Cymoril who leered at him and mocked him and whose face slowly aged until he saw a filthy crone and, ultimately, a skull on which the flesh rotted. He closed his eyes, but the image remained.

'Cymoril,' whispered the voices. *'Cymoril,'*

And Elric grew weaker as he became more desperate. He cried out for Dyvim Tvar, but heard only a mocking echo of the name, as he had heard Cymoril's. He shut his lips and he shut his eyes and, still crawling, tried to free himself from the groaning mist. But hours seemed to pass before the groans became whines and the whines became faint strands of sound and he tried to rise, opening his eyes to see the mist fading, but then his legs buckled and he fell down against the first step which led to the Ruby Throne. Again he had ignored Cymoril's advice concerning her brother—and again she was in danger. Elric's last thought was a simple one:

'I am not fit to live,' he thought.

4

To Call the Chaos Lord

AS SOON AS he recovered from the blow which had knocked him unconscious and thus wasted even more time, Elric sent for Dyvim Tvar. He was eager for news. But Dyvim Tvar could report nothing. Yyrkoon had summoned sorcerous aid to free him, sorcerous aid to effect his escape. 'He must have had some magical means of leaving the island, for he could not have gone by ship,' said Dyvim Tvar.

'You must send out expeditions,' said Elric. 'Send a thousand detachments if you must. Send every man in Melniboné. Strive to wake the dragons that they might be used. Equip the golden battle-barges. Cover the world with our men if you must, but find Cymoril.'

'All those things I have already done,' said Dyvim Tvar, 'save that I have not yet found Cymoril.'

A month passed and Imrryrian warriors marched and rode through the Young Kingdoms seeking news of their renegade countrymen.

'I worried more for myself than for Cymoril and I called that "morality",' thought the albino. 'I tested my sensibilities, not my conscience.'

A second month passed and Imrryrian dragons sailed the skies to South and East, West and North, but though they flew across mountains, and seas, and forests and plains and, unwittingly, brought terror to many a city, they found no sign of Yyrkoon and his band.

'For, finally, one can only judge oneself by one's actions,' thought Elric. 'I have looked at what I have done, not at what I meant to do or thought I would like to do, and what I have done has, in the main, been foolish, destructive and with little point. Yyrkoon was right to despise me and that was why I hated him so.'

A fourth month came and Imrryrian ships stopped in remote ports and Imrryrian sailors questioned other travelers and explorers for news of Yyrkoon. But Yyrkoon's sorcery had been strong and none had seen him (or remembered seeing him).

'I must now consider the implications of all these thoughts,' said Elric to himself.

Wearily, the swiftest of the soldiers began to return to Melniboné, bearing their useless news. And as faith disappeared and hope faded, Elric's determination increased. He made himself strong, both physically and mentally. He experimented with new drugs which would increase his energy rather than replenish the energy he did not share with other men. He read much in the library, though this time he read only certain grimoires and he read those over and over again.

These grimoires were written in the High Speech of Melniboné—the ancient language of sorcery with which Elric's ancestors had been able to communicate with the supernatural beings they had summoned. And at last Elric was satisfied that he understood them fully, though what he read sometimes threatened to stop him in his present course of action.

And when he was satisfied—for the dangers of misunderstanding the implications of the things described in the grimoires were catastrophic—he slept for three nights in a drugged slumber.

And then Elric was ready. He ordered all slaves and servants from his quarters. He placed guards at the doors with instructions to admit no one, no matter how urgent their business. He cleared one great chamber of all furniture so that it was completely empty save for one grimoire which he had placed in the very centre of the room. Then he seated himself beside the book and began to think.

When he had meditated for more than five hours Elric took a brush and a jar of ink and began to paint both walls and floor with complicated symbols, some of which were so intricate that they seemed to disappear at an angle to the surface on which they had been laid. At last this was done and Elric spreadeagled himself in the very centre of his huge rune, face down, one hand upon his grimoire, the other (with the Actorios upon it) stretched palm down. The moon was full. A shaft of its light fell directly upon Elric's head, turning the hair to silver. And then the Summoning began.

Elric sent his mind into twisting tunnels of logic, across endless plains of ideas, through mountains of symbolism and endless universes of alternate truths; he sent his mind out further and further and as it went he sent with it the words which issued from his writhing lips—words that few of his contemporaries would understand, though their very sound would chill the blood of any listener. And his body heaved as he forced it to remain in its original position and from time to time a groan would escape him. And through all this a few words came again and again.

One of these words was a name. 'Arioch'.

Arioch, the patron demon of Elric's ancestors; one of the most powerful of all the Dukes of Hell,

who was called Knight of the Swords, Lord of the
Seven Darks, Lord of the Higher Hell and many
more names besides.

'Arioch!'

It was on Arioch whom Yyrkoon had called, asking the Lord of Chaos to curse Elric. It was Arioch
whom Yyrkoon had sought to summon to aid him in
his attempt upon the Ruby Throne. It was Arioch
who was known as the Keeper of the Two Black
Swords—the swords of unearthly manufacture and
infinite power which had once been wielded by emperors of Melniboné.

'Arioch! I summon thee.'

Runes, both rhythmic and fragmented, howled
now from Elric's throat. His brain had reached the
plane on which Arioch dwelt. Now it sought Arioch
himself.

'Arioch! It is Elric of Melniboné who summons
thee.'

Elric glimpsed an eye staring down at him. The
eye floated, joined another. The two eyes regarded
him.

'Arioch! My Lord of Chaos! Aid me!'

The eyes blinked—and vanished.

'Oh, Arioch! Come to me! Come to me! Aid me
and I will serve you!'

A silhouette that was not a human form, turned
slowly until a black, faceless head looked down
upon Elric. A halo of red light gleamed behind the
head.

Then that, too, vanished.

Exhausted, Elric let the image fade. His mind
raced back through plane upon plane. His lips no
longer chanted the runes and the names. He lay exhausted upon the floor of his chamber, unable to
move, in silence.

He was certain that he had failed.

There was a small sound. Painfully he raised his

weary head.

A fly had come into the chamber. It buzzed about erratically, seeming almost to follow the lines of the runes Elric had so recently painted.

The fly settled first upon one rune and then on another.

It must have come in through the window, thought Elric. He was annoyed by the distraction but still fascinated by it.

The fly settled on Elric's forehead. It was a large, black fly and its buzz was loud, obscene. It rubbed its forelegs together, and it seemed to be taking a particular interest in Elric's face as it moved over it. Elric shuddered, but he did not have the strength to swat it. When it came into his field of vision, he watched it. When it was not visible he felt its legs covering every inch of his face. Then it flew up and, still buzzing loudly, hovered a short distance from Elric's nose. And then Elric could see the fly's eyes and recognise something in them. They were the eyes—and yet not the eyes—he had seen on that other plane.

It began to dawn on him that this fly was no ordinary creature. It had features that were in some way faintly human.

The fly smiled at him.

From his hoarse throat and through his parched lips Elric was able to utter but one word:

'Arioch?'

And a beautiful youth stood where the fly had hovered. The beautiful youth spoke in a beautiful voice—soft and sympathetic and yet manly. He was clad in a robe that was like a liquid jewel and yet which did not dazzle Elric, for in some way no light seemed to come from it. There was a slender sword at the youth's belt and he wore no helm, but a circlet of red fire. His eyes were wise and his eyes were old and when they were looked at closely they could be seen to contain an ancient and confident evil.

'Elric.'

That was all the youth said, but it revived the albino so that he could raise himself to his knees.

'Elric.'

And Elric could stand. He was filled with energy.

The youth was taller, now, than Elric. He looked down at the Emperor of Melniboné and he smiled the smile that the fly had smiled. 'You alone are fit to serve Arioch. It is long since I was invited to this plane, but now that I am here I shall aid you, Elric. I shall become your patron. I shall protect you and give you strength and the source of strength, though master I be and slave you be.'

'How must I serve you, Duke Arioch?' Elric asked, having made a monstrous effort of self-control, for he was filled with terror by the implications of Arioch's words.

'You will serve me by serving yourself for the moment. Later a time will come when I shall call upon you to serve me in specific ways, but (for the moment) I ask little of you, save that you swear to serve me.'

Elric hesitated.

'You must swear that,' said Arioch reasonably, 'or I cannot help you in the matter of your cousin Yyrkoon or his sister Cymoril.'

'I swear to serve you,' said Elric. And his body was flooded with ecstatic fire and he trembled with joy and he fell to his knees.

'Then I can tell you that, from time to time, you can call on my aid and I will come if your need is truly desperate. I will come in whichever form is appropriate, or no form at all if that should prove appropriate. And now you may ask me one question before I depart.'

'I need the answers to two questions.'

'Your first question I cannot answer. I will not answer. You must accept that you have now sworn to serve me. I will not tell you what the future holds. But you need not fear, if you serve me well.'

'Then my second question is this: Where is Prince Yyrkoon.'

'Prince Yyrkoon is in the south, in a land of barbarians. By sorcery and by superior weapons and intelligence he has effected the conquest of two mean nations, one of which is called Oin and the other of which is called Yu. Even now he trains the men of Oin and the men of Yu to march upon Melniboné, for he knows that your forces are spread thinly across the earth, searching for him.'

'How has he hidden?'

'He has not. But he has gained possession of the Mirror of Memory—a magical device whose hiding place he discovered by his sorceries. Those who look into this mirror have their memories taken. The mirror contains a million memories: the memories of all who have looked into it. Thus anyone who ventures into Oin or Yu or travels by sea to the capital which serves both is confronted by the mirror and forgets that he has seen Prince Yyrkoon and his Imrryrians in those lands. It is the best way of remaining undiscovered.'

'It is.' Elric drew his brows together. 'Therefore it might be wise to consider destroying the mirror. But what would happen then, I wonder?'

Arioch raised his beautiful hand. 'Although I have answered further questions which are, one could argue, part of the same question, I will answer no more. It could be in your interest to destroy the mirror, but it might be better to consider other means of countering its effects, for it does, I remind you, contain many memories, some of which have been imprisoned for thousands of years. Now I must go. And you must go—to the lands of Oin and Yu which lie several months' journey from here, to the south and well beyond Lormyr. They are best reached by the Ship Which Sails Over Both Land and Sea. Farewell, Elric.'

And a fly buzzed for a moment upon the wall before vanishing.

Elric rushed from the room, shouting for his slaves.

5

The Ship Which Sails Over
Land and Sea

'AND HOW MANY dragons still sleep in the caverns?'
Elric paced the gallery overlooking the city. It was
morning, but no sun came through the dull clouds
which hung low upon the towers of the Dreaming
City. Imrryr's life continued unchanged in the streets
below, save for the absence of the majority of her
soldiers who had not yet returned home from their
fruitless quests and would not be home for many
months to come.

Dyvim Tvar leaned on the parapet of the gallery
and stared unseeingly into the streets. His face was
tired and his arms were folded on his chest as if he
sought to contain what was left of his strength.

'Two perhaps. It would take a great deal to wake
them and even then I doubt if they'd be useful to us.
What is this "Ship Which Sails Over Land and Sea"
which Arioch spoke of?'

'I've read of it before—in the Silver Grimoire and
in other tomes. A magic ship. Used by a Melnibonéan hero even before there was Melniboné and
the empire. But where it exists, and if it exists, I

do not know.'

'Who would know?' Dyvim Tvar straightened his back and turned it on the scene below.

'Arioch?' Elric shrugged. 'But he would not tell me.'

'What of your friends the Water Elementals. Have they not promised you aid? And would they not be knowledgeable in the matter of ships?'

Elric frowned, deepening the lines which now marked his face. 'Aye—Straasha might know. But I'm loath to call on his aid again. The Water Elementals are not the powerful creatures that the Lords of Chaos are. Their strength is limited and, moreover, they are inclined to be capricious, in the manner of the elements. What is more, Dyvim Tvar, I hesitate to use sorcery, save where absolutely imperative . . .'

'You are a sorcerer, Elric. You have but lately proved your greatness in that respect, involving the most powerful of all sorceries, the summoning of a Chaos Lord—and you still hold back? I would suggest, my lord king, that you consider such logic and that you judge it unsound. You decided to use sorcery in your pursuit of Prince Yyrkoon. The die is already cast. It would be wise to use sorcery now.'

'You cannot conceive of the mental and physical effort involved . . .'

'I can conceive of it, my lord. I am your friend. I do not wish to see you pained—and yet . . .'

'There is also the difficulty, Dyvim Tvar, of my physical weakness,' Elric reminded his friend. 'How long can I continue in the use of these overstrong potions that now sustain me? They supply me with energy, aye—but they do so by using up my few resources. I might die before I find Cymoril.'

'I stand rebuked.'

But Elric came forward and put his white hand on Dyvim Tvar's butter-coloured cloak. 'But what have

I to lose, eh? No. You are right. I am a coward to
hesitate when Cymoril's life is at stake. I repeat my
stupidities—the stupidities which first brought this
pass upon us all. I'll do it. Will you come with me to
the ocean?'

'Aye.'

Dyvim Tvar began to feel the burden of Elric's
conscience settling upon him also. It was a peculiar
feeling to come to a Melnibonéan and Dyvim Tvar
knew very well that he liked it not at all.

Elric had last ridden these paths when he and Cymoril were happy. It seemed a long age ago. He had
been a fool to trust that happiness. He turned his
white stallion's head towards the cliffs and the sea
beyond them. A light rain fell. Winter was descend-
ing swiftly on Melniboné.

They left their horses on the cliffs, lest they be disturbed by Elric's sorcery-working, and clambered
down to the shore. The rain fell into the sea. A mist
hung over the water little more than five ship lengths
from the beach. It was deathly still and, with the
tall, dark cliffs behind them and the wall of mist before them, it seemed to Dyvim Tvar that they had
entered a silent netherworld where might easily be
encountered the melancholy souls of those who, in
legend, had committed suicide by a process of slow
self-mutilation. The sound of the two men's boots
on shingle was loud and yet was at once muffled by
the mist which seemed to suck at noise and swallow
it greedily as if it sustained its life on sound.

'Now,' Elric murmured. He seemed not to notice
the brooding and depressive surroundings. 'Now I
must recall the rune which came so easily, unsum-
moned, to my brain not many months since.' He left
Dyvim Tvar's side and went down to the place where
the chill water lapped the land and there, carefully,
he seated himself, cross-legged. His eyes stared, un-

seeingly, into the mist.

To Dyvim Tvar the tall albino appeared to shrink as he sat down. He seemed to become like a vulnerable child and Dyvim's Tvar's heart went out to Elric as it might go out to a brave, nervous boy, and Dyvim Tvar had it in mind to suggest that the sorcery be done with and they seek the lands of Oin and Yu by ordinary means.

But Elric was already lifting his head as a dog lifts its head to the moon. And strange, thrilling words began to tumble from his lips and it became plain that, even if Dyvim Tvar did speak now, Elric would not hear him.

Dyvim Tvar was no stranger to the High Speech—as a Melnibonéan noble he had been taught it as a matter of course—but the words seemed nonetheless strange to him, for Elric used peculiar inflections and emphases, giving the words a special and secret weight and chanting them in a voice which ranged from bass groan to falsetto shriek. It was not pleasant to listen to such noises coming from a mortal throat and now Dyvim Tvar had some clear understanding of why Elric was reluctant to use sorcery. The Lord of the Dragon Caves, Melnibonéan though he was, found himself inclined to step backward a pace or two, even to retire to the cliff-tops and watch over Elric from there, and he had to force himself to hold his ground as the summoning continued.

For a good space of time the rune-chanting went on. The rain beat harder upon the pebbles of the shore and made them glisten. It dashed most ferociously into the still, dark sea, lashed about the fragile head of the chanting, pale-haired figure, and caused Dyvim Tvar to shiver and draw his cloak more closely about his shoulders.

'Straasha—Straasha—Straasha . . .'

The words mingled with the sound of the rain. They were now barely words at all but sounds which the wind might make or a language which the sea might speak.

'Straasha . . .'

Again Dyvim Tvar had the impulse to move, but this time he desired to go to Elric and tell him to stop, to consider some other means of reaching the lands of Oin and Yu.

'Straasha!'

There was a cryptic agony in the shout.

'Straasha!'

Elric's name formed on Dyvim Tvar's lips, but he found that he could not speak it.

'Straasha!'

The cross-legged figure swayed. The word became the calling of the wind through the Caverns of Time.

'Straasha!'

It was plain to Dyvim Tvar that the rune was, for some reason, not working and that Elric was using up all his strength to no effect. And yet there was nothing the Lord of the Dragon Caves could do. His tongue was frozen. His feet seemed frozen. His feet seemed frozen to the ground.

He looked at the mist. Had it crept closer to the shore? Had it taken on a strange, almost luminous, green tinge? He peered closely.

There was a massive disturbance of the water. The sea rushed up the beach. The shingle crackled. The mist retreated. Vague lights flickered in the air and Dyvim Tvar thought he saw the shining silhouette of a gigantic figure emerging from the sea and he realised that Elric's chant had ceased.

'King Straasha,' Elric was saying in something approaching his normal tone. 'You have come. I thank you.'

The silhouette spoke and the voice reminded Dyvim Tvar of slow, heavy waves rolling beneath a friendly sun.

'We elementals are concerned, Elric, for there are rumours that you have invited Chaos Lords back to your plane and the elementals have never loved the Lords of Chaos. Yet I know that if you have done this it is because you are fated to do it and therefore we hold no enmity against you.'

'The decision was forced upon me, King Straasha. There was no other decision I could make. If you are therefore reluctant to aid me, I shall understand that and call on you no more.'

'I will help you, though helping you is harder now, not for what happens in the immediate future but what is hinted will happen in years to come. Now you must tell me quickly how we of the water can be of service to you.'

'Do you know ought of the Ship Which Sails Over Land and Sea? I need to find that ship if I am to fulfil my vow to find my love, Cymoril.'

'I know much of that ship, for it is mine. Grome also lays claim to it. But it is mine. Fairly, it is mine.'

'Grome of the Earth?'

'Grome of the Land Below the Roots. Grome of the Ground and all that lives under it. My brother. Grome. Long since, even as we elementals count time. Grome and I built that ship so that we could travel between the realms of Earth and Water whenever we chose. But we quarrelled (may we be cursed for such foolishness) and we fought. There were earthquakes, tidal waves, volcanic eruptions, typhoons and battles in which all the elementals joined, with the result that new continents were flung up and old ones drowned. It was not the first time we had fought each other, but it was the last. And finally, lest we destroy each other completely, we made a peace. I gave Grome part of my domain and he gave me the Ship Which Sails Over Land and Sea. But he gave it somewhat unwillingly and thus it *sails the sea better than it sails the land, for Grome thwarts its progress whenever he can. Still, if the ship is of use to you, you shall have it.'*

'I thank you, King Straasha. Where shall I find it?'

'It will come. And now I grow weary, for the further from my own realm I venture, the harder it is to sustain my mortal form. Farewell, Elric—and be cautious. You have a greater power than you know and many would make use of it to their own ends.'

'Shall I wait here for the Ship Which Sails Over Land and Sea?'

'No . . .' the Sea King's voice was fading as his form faded. Grey mist drifted back where the silhouette and the green lights had been. The sea again was still. *'Wait. Wait in your tower . . . It will come . . .'*

A few wavelets lapped the shore and then it was as if the king of the Water Elementals had never been there at all. Dyvim Tvar rubbed his eyes. Slowly at first he began to move to where Elric still sat. Gently he bent down and offered the albino his hand. Elric looked up in some surprise. 'Ah, Dyvim Tvar. How much time has passed?'

'Some hours, Elric. It will soon be night. What little light there is begins to wane. We had best ride back for Imrryr.'

Stiffly Elric rose to his feet, with Dyvim Tvar's assistance. 'Aye . . .' he murmured absently. 'The Sea King said . . .'

'I heard the Sea King, Elric. I heard his advice and I heard his warning. You must remember to heed both. I like too little the sound of this magic boat. Like most things of sorcerous origin, the ship appears to have vices as well as virtues, like a double-bladed knife which you raise to stab your enemy and which, instead, stabs you . . .'

'That must be expected where sorcery is concerned. It was you who urged me on, my friend.'

'Aye,' said Dyvim Tvar almost to himself as he led the way up the cliff-path towards the horses. 'Aye. I have not forgotten that, my lord king.'

Elric smiled wanly and touched Dyvim Tvar's arm. 'Worry not. The summoning is over and now we have the vessel we need to take us swiftly to Prince Yyrkoon and the lands of Oin and Yu.'

'Let us hope so.' Dyvim Tvar was privately sceptical about the benefits they would gain from the Ship Which Sails Over Land and Sea. They reached the horses and he began to wipe the water off the flanks of his own roan. 'I regret,' he said, 'that we have once again allowed the dragons to expend their energy on a useless endeavour. With a squadron of my beasts, we could do much against Prince Yyrkoon. And it would be fine and wild, my friend, to ride the skies again, side by side, as we used to.'

'When all this is done and Princess Cymoril brought home, we shall do that,' said Elric, hauling himself wearily into the saddle of his white stallion. 'You shall blow the Dragon Horn and our dragon brothers will hear it and you and I shall sing the *Song of the Dragon Masters* and our goads shall flash as we straddle Flamefang and his mate Sweet-claw. Ah, that will be like the days of old Melni-boné, when we no longer equate freedom with power, but let the Young Kingdoms go their own way and be certain that they let us go ours!'

Dyvim Tvar pulled on his horse's reins. His brow was clouded. 'Let us pray that day will come, my lord. But I cannot help this nagging thought which tells me that Imrryr's days are numbered and that my own life nears its close . . .'

'Nonsense, Dyvim Tvar. You'll survive me. There's little doubt of that, though you be my elder.'

Dyvim Tvar said, as they galloped back through the closing day: 'I have two sons. Did you know that, Elric?'

'You have never mentioned them.'

'They are by old mistresses.'

'I am happy for you.'

'They are fine Melnibonéans.'

'Why do you mention this, Dyvim Tvar?' Elric tried to read his friend's expression.

'It is that I love them and would have them enjoy the pleasures of the Dragon Isle.'

'And why should they not?'

'I do not know.' Dyvim Tvar looked hard at Elric. 'I could suggest that it is your responsibility, the fate of my sons, Elric.'

'Mine?'

'It seems to me, from what I gathered from the Water Elemental's words, that your decisions could decide the fate of the Dragon Isle. I ask you to remember my sons, Elric.'

'I shall, Dyvim Tvar. I am certain they shall grow into superb Dragon Masters and that one of them shall succeed you as Lord of the Dragon Caves.'

'I think you miss my meaning, my lord emperor.'

And Elric looked solemnly at his friend and shook his head. 'I do not miss your meaning, old friend. But I think you judge me harshly if you fear I'll do ought to threaten Melniboné and all she is.'

'Forgive me, then.' Dyvim Tvar lowered his head. But the expression in his eyes did not change.

In Imrryr they changed their clothes and drank hot wine and had spiced food brought. Elric, for all his weariness, was in better spirits than he had been for many a month. And yet there was still a tinge of something behind his surface mood which suggested he encouraged himself to speak gaily and put vitality into his movements. Admittedly, thought Dyvim Tvar, the prospects had improved and soon they would be confronting Prince Yyrkoon. But the dan-

gers ahead of them were unknown, the pitfalls probably considerable. Still, he did not, out of sympathy
for his friend, want to dispel Elric's mood. He was
glad, in fact, that Elric seemed in a more positive
frame of mind. There was talk of the equipment
they would need in their expedition to the mysterious lands of Yu and Oin, speculation concerning
the capacity of the Ship Which Sails Over Land and
Sea—how many men it would take, what provisions
they should put aboard and so on.

When Elric went to his bed, he did not walk with
the dragging tiredness which had previously accompanied his step and again, bidding him goodnight,
Dyvim Tvar was struck by the same emotion which
had filled him on the beach, watching Elric begin his
rune. Perhaps it was not by chance that he had used
the example of his sons when speaking to Elric earlier that day, for he had a feeling that was almost
protective, as if Elric were a boy looking forward to
some treat which might not bring him the joy he expected.

Dyvim Tvar dismissed the thoughts, as best he
could, and went to his own bed. Elric might blame
himself for all that had occurred in the question of
Yyrkoon and Cymoril, but Dyvim Tvar wondered if
he, too, were not to blame in some part. Perhaps he
should have offered his advice more cogently—
more vehemently, even—earlier and made a
stronger attempt to influence the young emperor.
And then, in the Melnibonéan manner, he dismissed
such doubts and questions as pointless. There was
only one rule—seek pleasure however you would.
But had that always been the Melnibonéan way?
Dyvim Tvar wondered suddenly if Elric might not
have regressive rather than deficient blood. Could
Elric be a reincarnation of one of their most distant
ancestors? Had it always been in the Melnibonéan
character to think only of oneself and one's own

gratification?

And again Dyvim Tvar dismissed the questions. What use was there in questions, after all? The world was the world. A man was a man. Before he sought his own bed he went to visit both his old mistresses, waking them up and insisting that he see his sons, Dyvim Slorm and Dyvim Mav and when his sons, sleepy-eyed, bewildered, had been brought to him, he stared at them for a long while before sending them back. He had said nothing to either, but he had brought his brows together frequently and rubbed at his face and shaken his head and, when they had gone, had said to Niopal and Saramal, his mistresses, who were as bewildered as their offspring, 'Let them be taken to the Dragon Caves tomorrow and begin their learning.'

'So soon, Dyvim Tvar?' said Niopal.

'Aye. There's little time left, I fear.'

He would not amplify on this remark because he could not. It was merely a feeling he had. But it was a feeling that was growing almost to the point where it was becoming an obsession with him.

In the morning Dyvim Tvar returned to Elric's tower and found the emperor pacing the gallery above the city, asking eagerly for any news of a ship sighted off the coast of the island. But no such ship had been seen. Servants answered earnestly that if their emperor could describe the ship, it would be easier for them to know for what to look, but he could not describe the ship, and could only hint that it might not be seen on water at all, but might appear on land. He was all dressed up in his black war gear and it was plain to Dyvim Tvar that Elric was indulging in even larger quantities of the potions which replenished his blood. The crimson eyes gleamed with a hot vitality, the speech was rapid and the bone-white hands moved with unnatural speed when Elric made even the lightest gesture.

'Are you well this morning, my lord?' asked the Dragon Master.

'In excellent spirits, thank you, Dyvim Tvar.' Elric grinned. 'Though I'd feel even better if the Ship Which Sails Over Land and Sea were here now.' He went to the balustrade and leaned upon it, peering over the towers and beyond the city walls, looking first to the sea and then to the land. 'Where can it be? I wish that King Straasha had been able to be more specific.'

'I'll agree with that.' Dyvim Tvar, who had not breakfasted, helped himself from the variety of succulent foods laid upon the table. It was evident that Elric had eaten nothing.

Dyvim Tvar began to wonder if the volume of potions had not affected his old friend's brain; perhaps madness, brought about by his involvement with complicated sorcery, his anxiety for Cymoril, his hatred of Yyrkoon, had begun to overwhelm Elric.

'Would it not be better to rest and to wait until the ship is sighted?' he suggested quietly as he wiped his lips.

'Aye—there's reason in that,' Elric agreed. 'But I cannot. I have an urge to be off, Dyvim Tvar, to come face to face with Yyrkoon, to have my revenge on him, to be united with Cymoril again.'

'I understand that. Yet, still . . .'

Elric's laugh was loud and ragged. 'You fret like Tanglebones over my well-being. I do not need two nursemaids, Lord of the Dragon Caves.'

With an effort Dyvim Tvar smiled. 'You are right. Well, I pray that this magical vessel—what is that?' He pointed out across the island. 'A movement in yonder forest. As if the wind passes through it. But there is no sign of wind elsewhere.'

Elric followed his gaze. 'You are right. I wonder . . .'

And then they saw something emerge from the forest and the land itself seemed to ripple. It was something which glinted white and blue and black. It came closer.

'A sail,' said Dyvim Tvar. 'It is your ship, I think, my lord.'

'Aye,' Elric whispered, craning forward. 'My ship. Make yourself ready, Dyvim Tvar. By midday we shall be gone from Imrryr.'

6

What the Earth God Desired

THE SHIP WAS tall and slender and she was delicate.
Her rails, masts and bulwarks were exquisitely
carved and obviously not the work of a mortal
craftsman. Though built of wood, the wood was not
painted but naturally shone blue and black and
green and a kind of deep smoky red; and her rigging
was the colour of sea-weed and there were veins in
the planks of her polished deck, like the roots of
trees, and the sails on her three tapering masts were
as fat and white and light as clouds on a fine sum-
mer day. The ship was everything that was lovely in
nature; few could look upon her and not feel delighted, as they might be delighted upon sighting a
perfect view. In a word, the ship radiated harmony,
and Elric could think of no finer vessel in which to
sail against Prince Yyrkoon and the dangers of the
lands of Oin and Yu.

The ship sailed gently in the ground as if upon the
surface of a river and the earth beneath the keel rippled as if turned momentarily to water. Wherever
the keel of the ship touched, and a few feet around
it, this effect became evident, though, after the ship

had passed, the ground would return to its usual stable state. This was why the trees of the forest had swayed as the ship passed through them, parting before the keel as the ship sailed towards Imrryr.

The Ship Which Sails Over Land and Sea was not particularly large. Certainly she was considerably smaller than a Melnibonéan battle-barge and only a little bigger than a southern galley. But the grace of her; the curve of her line; the pride of her bearing—in these, she had no rival at all.

Already her gangplanks had been lowered down to the ground and she was being made ready for her journey. Elric, hands on his slim hips, stood looking up at King Straasha's gift. From the gates of the city wall slaves were bearing provisions and arms and carrying them up the gangways. Meanwhile Dyvim Tvar was assembling the Imrryrian warriors and assigning them their ranks and duties while on the expedition. There were not many warriors. Only half the available strength could come with the ship, for the other half must remain behind under the command of Admiral Magum Colim and protect the city. It was unlikely that there would be any large attack on Melniboné after the punishment meted out to the barbarian fleet, but it was wise to take precautions, particularly since Prince Yyrkoon had vowed to conquer Imrryr. Also, for some strange reason that none of the onlookers could divine, Dyvim Tvar had called for volunteers—veterans who shared a common disability—and made up a special detachment of these men who, so the onlookers thought, could be of no use at all on the expedition. Still, neither were they of use when it came to defending the city, so they might as well go. These veterans were led aboard first.

Last to climb the gangway was Elric himself. He walked slowly, heavily, a proud figure in his black armour, until he reached the deck. Then he turned, saluted his city, and ordered the gangplank raised.

Dyvim Tvar was waiting for him on the poop-deck. The Lord of the Dragon Caves had stripped off one of his gauntlets and was running his naked hand over the oddly coloured wood of the rail. 'This is not a ship made for war, Elric,' he said. 'I should not like to see it harmed.'

'How can it be harmed?' Elric asked lightly as Imr-ryian's began to climb the rigging and adjust the sails. 'Would Straasha let it be destroyed? Would Grome? Fear not for the Ship Which Sails Over Land and Sea, Dyvim Tvar. Fear only for our own safety and the success of our expedition. Now, let us consult the charts. Remembering Straasha's warning concerning his brother Grome, I suggest we travel by sea for as far as possible, calling in here . . .' he pointed to a sea-port on the western coast of Lormyr—'to get our bearings and learn what we can of the lands of Oin and Yu and how those lands are defended.'

'Few travellers have ever ventured beyond Lor-myr. It is said that the edge of the world lies not far from that country's most southerly borders.' Dyvim Tvar frowned. 'Could not this whole mission be a trap, I wonder? Arioch's trap? What if he is in league with Prince Yyrkoon and we have been com-pletely deceived into embarking upon an expedition which will destroy us?'

'I have considered that,' said Elric. 'But there is no other choice. We must trust Arioch.'

'I suppose we must.' Dyvim Tvar smiled ironi-cally. 'Another matter now occurs to me. How does the ship move? I saw no anchors we could raise and there are no tides that I know of that sweep across the land. The wind fills the sails—see.' It was true. The sails were billowing and the masts creaked slightly as they took the strain.

Elric shrugged and spread his hands. 'I suppose

we must tell the ship,' he suggested. 'Ship—we are ready to sail.'

Elric took some pleasure in Dyvim Tvar's expression of astonishment as, with a lurch, the ship began to move. It sailed smoothly, as over a calm sea, and Dyvim Tvar instinctively clutched the rail, shouting: 'But we are heading directly for the city wall!'

Elric crossed quickly to the centre of the poop where a large lever lay, horizontally attached to a ratchet which in turn was attached to a spindle. This was almost certainly the steering gear. Elric grasped the lever as one might grasp an oar and pushed it round a notch or two. Immediately the ship responded—and turned towards another part of the wall! Elric hauled back on the lever and the ship leaned, protesting a little as she yawed around and began to head out across the island. Elric laughed in delight. 'You see, Dyvim Tvar, it is easy? A slight effort of logic was all it took!'

'Nonetheless,' said Dyvim Tvar suspiciously, 'I'd rather we rode dragons. At least they are beasts and may be understood. But this sorcery, it troubles me.'

'Those are not fitting words for a noble of Melniboné!' Elric shouted above the sound of the wind in the rigging, the creaking of the ship's timbers, the slap of the great white sails.

'Perhaps not,' said Dyvim Tvar. 'Perhaps that explains why I stand beside you now, my lord.'

Elric darted his friend a puzzled look before he went below to find a helmsman whom he could teach how to steer the ship.

The ship sped swiftly over rocky slopes and up gorse-covered hills; she cut her way through forests and sailed grandly over grassy plains. She moved like a low-flying hawk which keeps close to the ground but progresses with incredible speed and accuracy as it searches for its prey, altering its course with an imperceptible flick of a wing. The soldiers

of Imrryr crowded her decks, gasping in amazement
at the ship's progress over the land, and manyof the
men had to be clouted back to their positions at the
sails or elsewhere about the ship. The huge warrior
who acted as bosun seemed the only member of the
crew unaffected by the miracle of the ship. He was
behaving as he would normally behave aboard one
of the golden battle-barges; going solidly about his
duties and seeing to it that all was done in a proper
seamanly manner. The helmsman Elric had selected
was, on the other hand, wide-eyed and somewhat
nervous of the ship he handled. You could see that
he felt he was, at any moment, going to be dashed
against a slab of rock or smash the ship apart in a
tangle of thick-trunked pines. He was forever wet-
ting his lips and wiping sweat from his brow, even
though the air was sharp and his breath steamed as it
left his throat. Yet he was a good helmsman and
gradually he became used to handling the ship,
though his movements were, perforce, more rapid,
for there was little time to deliberate upon a decision, the ship travelled with such speed over the
land. The speed was breathtaking; they sped more
swiftly than any horse—were swifter, even, than
Dyvim Tvar's beloved dragons. Yet the motion was
exhilarating, too, as the expressions on the faces of
all the Imrryrians told.

Elric's delighted laughter rang through the ship
and infected many another member of the crew.

'Well, if Grome of the Roots is trying to block our
progress, I hesitate to guess how fast we shall travel
when we reach water!' he called to Dyvim Tvar.

Dyvim Tvar had lost some of his earlier mood.
His long, fine hair streamed around his face as he
smiled at his friend. 'Aye—we shall all be whisked
off the deck and into the sea!'

And then, as if in answer to their words, the ship
began suddenly to buck and at the same time sway

from side to side, like a ship caught in powerful cross-currents. The helmsman went white and clung to his lever, trying to get the ship back under control. There came a brief, terrified yell and a sailor fell from the highest cross-tree in the main mast and crashed onto the deck, breaking every bone in his body. And then the ship swayed once or twice and the turbulence was behind them and they continued on their course.

Elric stared at the body of the fallen sailor. Suddenly the mood of gaiety left him completely and he gripped the rail in his black gauntleted hands and he gritted his strong teeth and his crimson eyes glowed and his lips curled in self-mockery. 'What a fool I am. What a fool I am to tempt the gods so!'

Still, though the ship moved almost as swiftly as it had done, there seemed to be something dragging at it, as if Grome's minions clung on to the bottom as barnacles might cling in the sea. And Elric sensed something around him in the air, something in the rustling of the trees through which they passed, something in the movement of the grass and the bushes and the flowers over which they crossed, something in the weight of the rocks, of the angle of the hills. And he knew that what he sensed was the presence of Grome of the Ground—Grome of the Land Below the Roots—Grome, who desired to own what he and his brother Straasha had once owned jointly, what they had had made as a sign of the unity between them and over which they had then fought. Grome wanted very much to take back the Ship Which Sails Over Land and Sea. And Elric, staring down at the black earth, became afraid.

7

King Grome

BUT AT LAST, with the land tugging at their keel, they
reached the sea, sliding into the water and gathering
speed with every moment, until Melniboné was gone
behind them and they were sighting the thick clouds
of steam which hung forever over the Boiling Sea.
Elric thought it unwise to risk even this magical vessel in those peculiar waters, so the vessel was turned
and headed for the coast of Lormyr, sweetest and
most tranquil of the Young Kingdom nations, and
the port of Ramasaz on Lormyr's western shore. If
the southern barbarians with whom they had so recently fought had been from Lormyr, Elric would
have considered making for some other port, but
the barbarians had almost certainly been from the
South-East on the far side of the continent, beyond
Pikarayd. The Lormyrians, under their fat, cautious King Fadan, were not likely to join a raid unless its success were completely assured. Sailing
slowly into Ramasaz, Elric gave instructions that
their ship be moored in a conventional way and
treated like any ordinary ship. It attracted attention,
nonetheless, for its beauty, and the inhabitants of

the port were astonished to find Melnibonéans crewing the vessel. Though Melnibonéans were disliked throughout the Young Kingdoms, they were also feared. Thus, outwardly at any rate, Elric and his men were treated with respect and were served reasonably good food and wine in the hostelries they entered.

In the largest of the waterfront inns, a place called *Heading Outward and Coming Safely Home Again,* Elric found a garrulous host who had, until he bought the inn, been a prosperous fisherman and who knew the southernmost shores reasonably well. He certainly knew the lands of Oin and Yu, but he had no respect for them at all.

'You think they could be massing for war, my lord.' He raised his eyebrows at Elric before hiding his face in his wine-mug. Wiping his lips, he shook his red head. "Then they must war against sparrows. Oin and Yu are barely nations at all. Their only halfway decent city is Dhoz-Kam—and that is shared between them, half being on one side of the River Ar and half being on the other. As for the rest of Oin and Yu—it is inhabited by peasants who are for the most part so ill-educated and superstition-ridden that they are poverty-striken. Not a potential soldier among 'em.'

'You've heard nothing of a Melnibonéan renegade who has conquered Oin and Yu and set about training these peasants to make war?' Dyvim Tvar leaned on the bar next to Elric. He sipped fastidiously from a thick cup of wine. 'Prince Yyrkoon is the renegade's name.'

'Is that whom you seek?' The innkeeper became more interested. 'A dispute between the Dragon Princes, eh?'

'That's our business,' said Elric haughtily.

'Of course, my lords.'

'You know nothing of a great mirror which steals

men's memories?' Dyvim Tvar asked.

'A magical mirror!' The innkeeper threw back his head and laughed heartily. 'I doubt if there's one decent mirror in the whole of Oin or Yu! No, my lords, I think you are misled if you fear danger from those lands!"

'Doubtless you are right,' said Elric, staring down into his own untasted wine. 'But it would be wise if we were to check for ourselves—and it would be in Lormyr's interests, too, if we were to find what we seek and warn you accordingly.'

'Fear not for Lormyr. We can deal easily with any silly attempt to make war from that quarter. But if you'd see for yourselves, you must follow the coast for three days until you come to a great bay. The River Ar runs into that bay and on the shores of the river lies Dhoz-Kam—a seedy sort of city, particularly for a capital serving two nations. The inhabitants are corrupt, dirty and disease-ridden, but fortunately they are also lazy and thus afford little trouble, especially if you keep a sword by you. When you have spent an hour in Dhoz-Kam, you will realise the impossibility of such folk becoming a menace to anyone else, unless they should get close enough to you to infect you with one of their several plagues!' Again the innkeeper laughed hugely at his own wit. As he ceased shaking, he added: 'Or unless you fear their navy. It consists of a dozen or so filthy fishing boats, most of which are so unseaworthy they dare only fish the shallows of the estuary.'

Elric pushed his wine-cup aside. 'We thank you, landlord.' He placed a Melnibonéan silver piece upon the counter.

'This will be hard to change,' said the innkeeper craftily.

'There is no need to change it on our account,' Elric told him.

'I thank you, masters. Would you stay the night at

my establishment. I can offer you the finest beds in Ramasaz.'

'I think not,' Elric told him. 'We shall sleep aboard out ship tonight, that we might be ready to sail at dawn.'

The landlord watched the Melnibonéans depart. Instinctively he bit at the silver piece and then, suspecting he tasted something odd about it, removed it from his mouth. He stared at the coin, turning it this way and that. Could Melnibonéan silver be poisonous to an ordinary mortal? he wondered. It was best not to take risks. He tucked the coin into his purse and collected up the two wine-cups they had left behind. Though he hated waste, he decided it would be wiser to throw the cups out lest they should have become tainted in some way.

The Ship Which Sails Over Land and Sea reached the bay at noon on the following day and now it lay close inshore, hidden from the distant city by a short isthmus on which grew thick, near-tropical foliage. Elric and Dyvim Tvar waded through the clear, shallow water to the beach and entered the forest. They had decided to be cautious and not make their presence known until they had determined the truth of the innkeeper's contemptuous description of Dhoz-Kam. Near the tip of the isthmus was a reasonably high hill and growing on the hill were several good-sized trees. Elric and Dyvim Tvar used their swords to clear a path through the undergrowth and made their way up the hill until they stood under the trees, picking out the one most easily climbed. Elric selected a tree whose trunk bent and then straightened out again. He sheathed his sword, got his hands onto the trunk and hauled himself up, clambering along until he reached a succession of thick branches which would bear his weight. In the meantime Dyvim Tvar climbed another nearby tree until at last both men could get a good view across the bay where the city of Dhoz-Kam could be clearly seen. Certainly the city itself deserved the innkeeper's description. It was squat and grimy and evidently poor. Doubtless this was why Yyrkoon had chosen it, for the lands of Oin and Yu could not have been hard to conquer with the help of a handful of well-trained Imrryrians and some of Yyrkoon's sorcerous allies. Indeed, few would have bothered to conquer such a place, since its wealth was plainly virtually non-existent and its geographical position of no strategic importance. Yyrkoon had chosen well, for purposes of secrecy if nothing else. But the landlord had been wrong about Dhoz-Kam's fleet. Even from here Elric and Dyvim Tvar could make out a good thirty good-sized warships in the harbour and there seemed to be more anchored up-river. But the ships did not interest them as much as the thing which flashed and glittered above the city— something which had been mounted on huge pillars which supported an axle which, in turn, supported a vast, circular mirror set in a frame whose workmanship was as plainly non-mortal as that of the ship which had brought the Melnibonéans here. There was no doubt that they looked upon the Mirror of Memory and that any who had sailed into the harbour after it had been erected must have had their memory of what they had seen stolen from them instantly.

'It seems to me, my lord,' said Dyvim Tvar from his perch a yard or two away from Elric, 'that it would be unwise of us to sail directly into the harbour of Dhoz-Kam. Indeed, we could be in danger if we entered the bay. I think that we look upon the mirror, even now, only because it is not pointed directly at us. But you notice there is machinery to turn it in any direction its user chooses—save one. It cannot be turned inland, behind the city. There is no need for it, for who would approach Oin and Yu from the wastelands beyond their borders and who but the inhabitants of Oin or Yu would need to come overland to their capital?'

'I think I take your meaning, Dyvim Tvar. You suggest that we would be wise to make use of the special properties of our ship and . . .'

'. . . and go overland to Dhoz-Kam, striking suddenly and making full use of those veterans we brought with us, moving swiftly and ignoring Prince Yyrkoon's new allies—seeking the prince himself, and his renegades. Could we do that, Elric? Dash into the city—seize Yyrkoon, rescue Cymoril—then speed out again and away?'

'Since we have too few men to make a direct assault, it is all we can do, though it's dangerous. The advantage of surprise would be lost, of course, once we had made the attempt. If we failed in our first attempt it would become much harder to attack a second time. The alternative is to sneak into the city at night and hope to locate Yyrkoon and Cymoril alone, but then we should not be making use of our one important weapon, the Ship Which Sails Over Land and Sea. I think your plan is the best one, Dyvim Tvar. Let us turn the ship inland, now, and hope that Grome takes his time in finding us—for I still worry lest he try seriously to wrest the ship from our possession.' Elric began to climb down towards the ground.

Standing once more upon the poop-deck of the lovely ship, Elric ordered the helmsman to turn the vessel once again towards the land. Under half-sail the ship moved gracefully through the water and up the curve of the bank and the flowering shrubs of the forest parted before its prow and then they were sailing through the green dark of the jungle, while startled birds cawed and shrilled and little animals paused in astonishment and peered down from the trees at the Ship Which Sails Over Land and Sea and some almost lost their balance as the graceful boat progressed calmly over the floor of the forest, turning aside for only the thickest of the trees.

And thus they made their way to the interior of the land called Oin, which lay to the north of the River Ar, which marked the border between Oin and the land called Yu with which Oin shared a single capital.

Oin was a country consisting largely of unforested jungle and infertile plains where the inhabitants farmed, for they feared the forest and would not go into it, even though that was where Oin's wealth might be found.

The ship sailed well enough through the forest and out over the plain and soon they could see a large lake glinting ahead of them and Dyvim Tvar, glancing at the crude map with which he had furnished himself in Ramasaz, suggested that they begin to turn towards the south again and approach Dhoz-Kam by means of a wide semi-circle. Elric agreed and the ship began to tack round.

It was then that the land began to heave again and huge waves of grassy earth this time rolled around the ship and blotted out the surrounding view. The ship pitched wildly up and down and from side to side. Two more Imrryrians fell from the rigging and were killed on the deck below. The bosun was shouting loudly—though in fact all this upheaval was happening in silence—and the silence made the situation seem that much more menacing. The bosun yelled to his men to tie themselves to their positions. 'And all those not doing anything—get below at once!' he added.

Elric had wound a scarf around the rail and tied the other end to his wrist. Dyvim Tvar had used a long belt for the same purpose. But still they were

flung in all directions, often losing their footing as
the ship bucked this way and that, and every bone in
Elric's body seemed about to crack and every inch of
his flesh seemed bruised. And the ship was creaking
and protesting and threatening to break up under
the awful strain of riding the heaving land.

'Is this Grome's work, Elric?' Dyvim Tvar
panted. 'Or is it some sorcery of Yyrkoon's?'

Elric shook his head. 'Not Yyrkoon. It is Grome.
And I know no way to placate him. Not Grome,
who thinks least of all the Kings of the Elements,
yet, perhaps, is the most powerful.'

'But surely he breaks his bargain with his brother
by doing this to us?'

'No. I think not. King Straasha warned us this
might happen. We can only hope that Grome ex-
pends all his energy and that the ship survives, as it
might survive a natural storm at sea.'

'This is worse than a sea-storm, Elric!'

Elric nodded his agreement but could say nothing, for the deck was tilting at a crazy angle and he
had to cling to the rails with both hands in order to
retain any kind of footing.

And now the silence stopped.

Instead they heard a rumbling and a roaring that
seemed to have something of the character of laughter.

'King Grome!' Elric shouted. 'King Grome! Let
us be! We have done you no harm!'

But the laughter increased and it made the whole
ship quiver as the land rose and fell around it, as
trees and hills and rocks rushed towards the ship and
then fell away again, never quite engulfing them, for
Grome doubtless wanted his ship intact.

'Grome! You have no quarrel with mortals!' Elric
cried again. 'Let us be! Ask a favour of us if you
must, but grant us this favour in return!'

Elric was shouting almost anything that came into

his head. Really, he had no hope of being heard by the earth god and he did not expect King Grome to bother to listen even if the elemental did hear. But there was nothing else to do.

'Grome! Grome! Grome! Listen to me!'

Elric's only response was in the louder laughter which made every nerve in him tremble. And the earth heaved higher and dropped lower and the ship spun round and round until Elric was sure he would lose his senses entirely.

'King Grome! King Grome! Is it just to slay those who have never done you harm?'

And then, slowly, the heaving earth subsided and the ship was still and a huge, brown figure stood looking down at the ship. The figure was the colour of earth and looked like a vast, old oak. His hair and his beard were the colour of leaves and his eyes were the colour of gold ore and his teeth were the colour of granite and his feet were like roots and his skin seemed covered in tiny green shoots in place of hair and he smelled rich and musty and good and he was King Grome of the Earth Elementals. He sniffed and he frowned and he said in a soft, mighty voice that was yet coarse and grumpy: 'I want my ship.'

'It is not our ship to give, King Grome,' said Elric.

Grome's tone of petulance increased. 'I want my ship,' he said slowly. 'I want the thing. It is mine.'

'Of what use is it to you, King Grome?'

'Use? It is mine.'

Grome stamped and the land rippled.

Elric said desperately: 'It is your brother's ship, King Grome. It is King Straasha's ship. He gave you part of his domain and you allowed him to keep the ship. That was the bargain.'

'I know nothing of a bargain. The ship is mine.'

'You know that if you take the ship then King Straasha will have to take back the land he gave you.'

'I want my ship.' The huge figure shifted its position and bits of earth fell from it, landing with distinctly heard thuds on the ground below and on the deck of the ship.

'Then you must kill us to obtain it,' Elric said.

'Kill? Grome does not kill mortals. He kills nothing. Grome builds. Grome brings to life.'

'You have already killed three of our company,' Elric pointed out. 'Three are dead, King Grome, because you made the land-storm.'

Grome's great brows drew together and he scratched his great head, causing an immense rustling noise to sound. 'Grome does not kill,' he said again.

'King Grome has killed,' said Elric reasonably. 'Three lives lost.'

Grome grunted. 'But I want my ship.'

'The ship is lent to us by your brother. We cannot give it to you. Besides, we sail in it for a purpose—a noble purpose, I think. We . . .'

'I know nothing of "purposes"—and care nothing for you. I want my ship. My brother should not have lent it to you. I had almost forgotten it. But now that I remember it, I want it.'

'Will you not accept something else in place of the ship, King Grome?' said Dyvim Tvar suddenly. 'Some other gift.'

Grome shook his monstrous head. 'How could a mortal give me something? It is mortals who take from me all the time. They steal my bones and my blood and my flesh. Could you give me back all that your kind has taken?'

'Is there not one thing?' Elric said.

Grome closed his eyes.

'Precious metals? Jewels?' suggested Dyvim Tvar. 'We have many such in Melniboné.'

'I have plenty,' said King Grome.

Elric shrugged in despair. 'How can we bargain

with a god, Dyvim Tvar?' He gave a bitter smile.
'What can the Lord of the Soil desire? More sun,
more rain? These are not ours to give.'

'I am a rough sort of god,' said Grome, 'if indeed
god I am. But I did not mean to kill your comrades.
I have an idea. Give me the bodies of the slain. Bury
them in my earth.'

Elric's heart leapt. 'That is all you wish of us.'

'It would seem much to me.'

'And for that you will let us sail on?'

'On water, aye,' growled Grome. 'But I do not see
why I should allow you to sail over my land. It is too
much to expect of me. You can go to yonder lake,
but from now this ship will only possess the properties bestowed upon it by my brother Straasha. No
longer shall it cross my domain.'

'But, King Grome, we need this ship. We are upon
urgent business. We need to sail to the city yonder.'
Elric pointed in the direction of Dhoz-Kam.

'You may go to the lake, but after that the ship
will sail only on water. Now give me what I ask.'

Elric called down to the bosun who, for the first
time, seemed amazed by what he was witnessing.
'Bring up the bodies of the three dead men.'

The bodies were brought up from below. Grome
stretched out one of his great, earthy hands and
picked them up.

'I thank you,' he growled. 'Farewell.'

And slowly Grome began to descend into the
ground, his whole huge frame becoming, atom by
atom, absorbed with the earth until he was gone.

And then the ship was moving again, slowly towards the lake, on the last short voyage it would
ever make upon the land.

'And thus our plans are thwarted,' said Elric.

Dyvim Tvar looked miserably towards the shining lake. 'Aye. So much for that scheme. I hesitate
to suggest this to you, Elric, but I fear we must re-

sort to sorcery again if we are to stand any chance of achieving our goal.'

Elric sighed.

'I fear we must,' he said.

8

The City and the Mirror

PRINCE YYRKOON WAS pleased. His plans went well.
He peered through the high fence which enclosed
the flat roof of his house (three storeys high and the
finest in Dhoz-Kam); he looked out towards the harbour at his splendid, captured fleet. Every ship
which had come to Dhoz-Kam and which had not
flown the standard of a powerful nation had been
easily taken after its crew had looked upon the great
mirror which squatted on its pillars above the city.
Demons had built those pillars and Prince Yyrkoon
had paid them for their work with the souls of all
those in Oin and Yu who had resisted him. Now
there was one last ambition to fulfil and then he and
his new followers would be on their way to Melniboné . . .

He turned and spoke to his sister. Cymoril lay on
a wooden bench, staring unseeingly at the sky, clad
in the filthy tatters of the dress she had been wearing
when Yyrkoon abducted her from her tower.

'See our fleet, Cymoril! While the golden barges
are scattered we shall sail unhampered into Imrryr
and declare the city ours. Elric cannot defend him-

self against us now. He fell so easily into my trap. He is a fool! And you were a fool to give him your affection!'

Cymoril made no response. Through all the months she had been away, Yyrkoon had drugged her food and drink and produced in her a lassitude which rivalled Elric's undrugged condition. Yyrkoon's own experiments with his sorcerous powers had turned him gaunt, wild-eyed and some-what mangy; he ceased to take any pains with his physical appearance. But Cymoril had a wasted, haunted look to her, for all that beauty remained. It was as if Dhoz-Kam's rundown seediness had infected them both in different ways.

'Fear not for your own future, however, my sister,' Yyrkoon continued. He chuckled. 'You shall still be empress and sit beside the emperor on his Ruby Throne. Only I shall be emperor and Elric shall die for many days and the manner of his death will be more inventive than anything he thought to do to me.'

Cymoril's voice was hollow and distant. She did not turn her head when she spoke. 'You are insane, Yyrkoon.'

'Insane? Come now, sister, is that a word that a true Melnibonéan should use? We Melnibonéans judge nothing sane or insane. What a man is—he is. What he does—he does. Perhaps you have stayed too long in the Young Kingdoms and its judgments are becoming yours. But that shall soon be righted. We shall return to the Dragon Isle in triumph and you will forget all this, just as if you yourself had looked into the Mirror of Memory.' He darted a nervous glance upwards, as if he half-expected the mirror to be turned on him.

Cymoril closed her eyes. Her breathing was heavy and very slow; she was bearing this nightmare with fortitude, certain that Elric must eventually rescue her from it. That hope was all that had stopped her from destroying herself. If the hope went altogether, then she would bring about her own death and be done with Yyrkoon and all his horrors.

'Did I tell you that last night I was successful? I raised demons, Cymoril. Such powerful, dark demons. I learned from them all that was left for me to learn. And I opened the Shade Gate at last. Soon I shall pass through it and there I shall find what I seek. I shall become the most powerful mortal on earth. Did I tell you all this, Cymoril?'

He had, in fact, repeated himself several times that morning, but Cymoril had paid no more attention to him than she did now. She felt so tired. She tried to sleep. She said slowly, as if to remind herself of something: 'I hate you, Yyrkoon.'

'Ah, but you shall love me soon, Cymoril. Soon.'

'Elric will come . . .'

'Elric! Ha! He sits twiddling his thumbs in his tower, waiting for news that will never come—save when I bring it to him!'

'Elric will come,' she said.

Yyrkoon snarled. A brute-faced Oinish girl brought him his morning wine. Yyrkoon seized the cup and sipped the stuff. Then he spat it at the girl who, trembling, ducked away. Yyrkoon took the jug and emptied it onto the white dust of the roof. 'This is Elric's thin blood. This is how it will flow away!'

But again Cymoril was not listening. She was trying to remember her albino lover and the few sweet days they had spent together since they were children.

Yyrkoon hurled the empty jug at the girl's head, but she was adept at dodging him. As she dodged, she murmured her standard response to all his attacks and insults. 'Thank you, Demon Lord,' she said. 'Thank you, Demon Lord.'

Yyrkoon laughed. 'Aye. Demon Lord. Your folk

are right to call me that, for I rule more demons than I rule men. My power increases every day!'

The Oinish girl hurried away to fetch more wine, for she knew he would be calling for it in a moment. Yyrkoon crossed the roof to stare through the slats in the fence at the proof of his power, but as he looked upon his ships he heard sounds of confusion from the other side of the roof. Could the Yurits and the Oinish be fighting amongst themselves? Where were their Imrryrian centurions. Where was Captain Valharik?

He almost ran across the roof, passing Cymoril who appeared to be sleeping, and peered down into the streets.

'Fire?' he murmured. 'Fire?'

It was true that the streets appeared to be on fire. And yet it was not an ordinary fire. Balls of fire seemed to drift about, igniting rush-thatched roofs, doors, anything which would easily burn—as an invading army might put a village to the torch.

Yyrkoon scowled, thinking at first that he had been careless and some spell of his had turned against him, but then he looked over the burning houses at the river and he saw a strange ship sailing there, a ship of great grace and beauty, that somehow seemed more a creation of nature than of man—and he knew they were under attack. But who would attack Dhoz-Kam? There was no loot worth the effort. It could not be Imrryrians . . .

It could not be Elric.

'It must not be Elric,' he growled. 'The Mirror. It must be turned upon the invaders.'

'And upon yourself, brother?' Cymoril had risen unsteadily and leaned against a table. She was smiling. 'You were too confident, Yyrkoon. Elric comes.'

'Elric! Nonsense! Merely a few barbarian raiders from the interior. Once they are in the centre of the city, we shall be able to use the Mirror of Memory upon them.' He ran to the trapdoor which led down into his house. 'Captain Valharik! Valharik where are you?'

Valharik appeared in the room below. He was sweating. There was a blade in his gloved hand, though he did not seem to have been in any fighting as yet.

'Make the mirror ready, Valharik. Turn it upon the attackers.'

'But, my lord, we might . . .'

'Hurry! Do as I say. We'll soon have these barbarians added to our own strength—along with their ships.'

'Barbarians, my lord? Can barbarians command the fire elementals? These things we fight are flame spirits. They cannot be slain any more than fire itself can be slain.'

'Fire can be slain by water,' Prince Yyrkoon reminded his lieutenant. 'By water, Captain Valharik. Have you forgotten?'

'But, Prince Yyrkoon, we have tried to quench the spirits with water—and the water will not move from our buckets. Some powerful sorcerer commands the invaders. He has the aid of the spirits of fire *and* water.'

'You are mad, Captain Valharik,' said Yyrkoon firmly. 'Mad. Prepare the mirror and let us have no more of these stupidities.'

Valharik wetted his dry lips. 'Aye, my lord.' He bowed his head and went to do his master's bidding.

Again Yyrkoon went to the fence and looked through. There were men in the streets now, fighting his own warriors, but smoke obscured his view, he could not make out the identities of any of the invaders. 'Enjoy your petty victory,' Yyrkoon chuckled, 'for soon the mirror will take away your minds and you will become my slaves.'

'It is Elric,' said Cymoril quietly. She smiled. 'Elric comes to take vengeance on you, brother.'

Yyrkoon sniggered. 'Think you? Think you? Well, should that be the case, he'll find me gone, for I still have a means of evading him—and he'll find you in a condition which will not please him (though it will cause him considerable anguish). But it is not Elric. It is some crude shaman from the steppes to the east of here. He will soon be in my power.'

Cymoril, too, was peering through the fence.

'Elric,' she said. 'I can see his helm.'

'What?' Yyrkoon pushed her aside. There, in the streets, Imrryrian fought Imrryrian, there was no longer any doubt of that. Yyrkoon's men— Imrryrian, Oinish and Yurit—were being pushed back. And at the head of the attacking Imrryrians could be seen a black dragon helm such as only one Melnibonéan wore. It was Elric's helm. And Elric's sword, that had once belonged to Earl Aubec of Malador, rose and fell and was bright with blood which glistened in the morning sunshine.

For a moment Yyrkoon was overwhelmed with despair. He groaned. 'Elric. Elric. Elric. Ah, how we continue to underestimate each other. What curse is on us?'

Cymoril had flung back her head and her face had come to life again. 'I said he would come, brother!'

Yyrkoon whirled on her. 'Aye—he has come— and the mirror will rob him of his brain and he will turn into my slave, believing anything I care to put in his skull. This is even sweeter than I planned, sister. Ha!' He looked up and then flung his arms across his eyes as he realised what he had done. 'Quickly—below—into the house—the mirror begins to turn.' There came a great creaking of gears and pulleys and chains as the terrible Mirror of Memory began to focus on the streets below. 'It will be only a little while before Elric has added himself and his men to my strength. What a splendid irony!' Yyrkoon hurried his sister down the steps leading from the roof and he closed the trapdoor behind him. 'Elric himself will help in the attack on Imrryr. He will destroy his own kind. He will oust himself from the Ruby Throne!'

'Do you not think that Elric has anticipated the threat of the Mirror of Memory, brother?' Cymoril said with relish.

'Anticipate it, aye—but resist it he cannot. He must see to fight. He must either be cut down or open his eyes. No man with eyes can be safe from the power of the mirror.' He glanced around the crudely furnished room. 'Where is Valharik? Where is the cur?'

Valharik came running in. 'The mirror is being turned, my lord, but it will affect our own men, too. I fear . . .'

'Then cease to fear. What if our own men are drawn under its influence? We can soon feed what they need to know back into their brains—at the same time as we feed our defeated foes. You are too nervous, Captain Valharik.'

'But Elric leads them . . .'

'And Elric's eyes *are* eyes—though they look like crimson stones. He will fare no better than his men.'

In the streets around Prince Yyrkoon's house Elric, Dyvim Tvar and their Imrryrians pushed on, forcing back their demoralised opponents. The attackers had lost barely a man, whereas many Oinish and Yurits lay dead in the streets, beside a few of their renegade Imrryrian commanders. The flame elementals, whom Elric had summoned with some effort, were beginning to disperse, for it cost them dear to spend so much time entirely within Elric's plane, but the necessary advantage had been gained and there was now little question of who would win as a hundred or more houses blazed throughout the city, igniting others and requiring attention from the defenders lest the whole squalid place burn down about their ears. In the harbour, too, ships were burning.

Dyvim Tvar was the first to notice the mirror beginning to swing into focus on the streets. He pointed a warning finger, then turned, blowing on his war-horn and ordering forward the troops who, up to now, had played no part in the fighting. 'Now you must lead us!' he cried, and he lowered his helm over his face. The eyeholes of the helm had been blocked so that he could not see through.

Slowly Elric lowered his own helm until he was in darkness. The sound of fighting continued however, as the veterans who had sailed with them from Melniboné, set to work in their place and the other troops fell back. The leading Imrryrians had not blocked their eyeholes.

Elric prayed that the scheme would work.

Yyrkoon, peeking cautiously through a chink in a heavy curtain, said querulously: 'Valharik? They fight on. Why is that? Is not the mirror focussed?'

'It should be, my lord.'

'Then, see for yourself, the Imrryrians continue to forge through our defenders—and our men are beginning to come under the influence of the mirror. What is wrong, Valharik? What is wrong?'

Valharik drew air between his teeth and there was a certain admiration in his expression as he looked upon the fighting Imrryrians.

'They are blind,' he said. 'They fight by sound and touch and smell. They are blind, my lord emperor—and they lead Elric and his men whose helms are so designed they can see nothing.'

'Blind?' Yyrkoon spoke almost pathetically, refusing to understand. 'Blind?'

'Aye. Blind warriors—men wounded in earlier wars, but good fighters nonetheless. That is how Elric defeats our mirror, my lord.'

'Agh! No! No!' Yyrkoon beat heavily on his captain's back and the man shrank away. 'Elric is not cunning. He is not cunning. Some powerful demon gives him these ideas.'

'Perhaps, my lord. But are there demons more powerful than those who have aided you?'

'No,' said Yyrkoon. 'There are none. Oh, that I could summon some of them now. But I have expended my powers in opening the Shade Gate. I should have anticipated . . . I could not anticipate . . . Oh Elric! I shall yet destroy you, when the runeblades are mine!' Then Yyrkoon frowned. 'But how could he have been prepared? What demon . . . ? Unless he summoned Arioch himself? But he has not the power to summon Arioch. I could not summon him . . ."

And then, as if in reply, Yyrkoon heard Elric's battle song sounding from the nearby streets. And that song answered the question.

'Arioch! Arioch! Blood and souls for my lord Arioch!'

'Then I must have the runeblades. I must pass through the Shade Gate. There I still have allies—supernatural allies who shall deal easily with Elric, if need be. But I need time . . .' Yyrkoon mumbled to himself as he paced about the room. Valharik continued to watch the fighting.

'They come closer,' said the captain.

Cymoril smiled. 'Closer, Yyrkoon? Who is the fool now? Elric? Or you?'

'Be still! I think. I think . . .' Yyrkoon fingered his lips.

Then a light came into his eye and he looked cunningly at Cymoril for a second before turning his attention to Captain Valharik.

'Valharik, you must destroy the Mirror of Memory.'

'Destroy it? But it is our only weapon, my lord?'

'Exactly—but is it not useless now?'

'Aye.'

'Destroy it and it will serve us again.' Yyrkoon flicked a long finger in the direction of the door. 'Go. Destroy the mirror.'

'But, Prince Yyrkoon—emperor, I mean—will that not have the effect of robbing us of our only weapon?'

'Do as I say, Valharik! Or perish!'

'But how shall I destroy it, my lord?'

'Your sword. You must climb the column *behind* the face of the mirror. Then, without looking into the mirror itself, you must swing your sword against it and smash it. It will break easily. You know the precautions I have had to take to make sure that it was not harmed.'

'Is that all I must do?'

'Aye. Then you are free from my service—you may escape or do whatever else you wish to do.'

'Do we not sail against Melniboné?'

'Of course not. I have devised another method of taking the Dragon Isle.'

Valharik shrugged. His expression showed that he had never really believed Yyrkoon's assurances. But what else had he to do but follow Yyrkoon, when fearful torture awaited him at Elric's hands? With shoulders bowed, the captain slunk away to do his prince's work.

'And now, Cymoril . . .' Yyrkoon grinned like a ferret as he reached out to grab his sister's soft shoulders. 'Now to prepare you for your lover, Elric.'

One of the blind warriors cried: 'They no longer re-

sist us, my lord. They are limp and allow themselves
to be cut down where they stand. Why is this?'

'The mirror has robbed them of their memories,'
Elric called, turning his own blind head towards the
sound of the warrior's voice. 'You can lead us into a
building now—where, with luck, we shall not
glimpse the mirror.'

At last they stood within what appeared to Elric,
as he lifted his helm, to be a warehouse of some
kind. Luckily it was large enough to hold their entire
force and when they were all inside Elric had the
doors shut while they debated their next action.

'We should find Yyrkoon,' Dyvim Tvar said. 'Let
us interrogate one of those warriors . . .'

'There'll be little point in that, my friend,' Elric
reminded him. 'Their minds are gone. They'll remember nothing at all. They do not at present remember even what they are, let alone who. Go to the
shutters yonder, where the mirror's influence cannot
reach, and see if you can see the building most likely
to be occupied by my cousin.'

Dyvim Tvar crossed swiftly to the shutters and
looked cautiously out. 'Aye—there's a building
larger than the rest and I see some movement
within, as if the surviving warriors were regrouping.
It's likely that's Yyrkoon's stronghold. It should be
easily taken.'

Elric joined him. 'Aye. I agree with you. We'll
find Yyrkoon there. But we must hurry, lest he de-
cides to slay Cymoril. We must work out the best
means of reaching the place and instruct our blind
warriors as to how many streets, how many houses
and so forth, we must pass.'

'What is that strange sound?' One of the blind
warriors raised his head. 'Like the distant ringing of
a gong.'

'I hear it too,' said another blind man.

And now Elric heard it. A sinister noise. It came

from the air above them. It shivered through the atmosphere.

'The mirror!' Dyvim Tvar looked up. 'Has the mirror some property we did not anticipate?'

'Possibly . . .' Elric tried to remember what Arioch had told him. But Arioch had been vague. He had said nothing of this dreadful, mighty sound, this shattering clangour as if . . . 'He is breaking the mirror!' he said. 'But why?' There was something more now, something brushing at his brain. As if the sound were, itself, sentient.

'Perhaps Yyrkoon is dead and his magic dies with him,' Dyvim Tvar began. And then he broke off with a groan.

The noise was louder, more intense, bringing sharp pain to his ears.

And now Elric knew. He blocked his ears with his gauntleted hands. The memories in the mirror. They were flooding into his mind. The mirror had been smashed and was releasing all the memories it had stolen over the centuries—the aeons, perhaps. Many of those memories were not mortal. Many were the memories of beasts and intelligent creatures which had existed even before Melniboné. And the memories warred for a place in Elric's skull—in the skulls of all the Imrryrians—in the poor, tortured skulls of the men outside whose pitiful screams could be heard rising from the streets—and in the skull of Captain Valharik, the turncoat, as he lost his footing on the great column and fell with the shards from the mirror to the ground far below.

But Elric did not hear Captain Valharik scream and he did not hear Valharik's body crash first to a roof-top and then into the street where it lay all broken beneath the broken mirror.

Elric lay upon the stone floor of the warehouse and he writhed, as his comrades writhed, trying to

clear his head of a million memories that were not
his own—of loves, of hatreds, of strange experiences and ordinary experiences, of wars and jour-
neys, of the faces of relatives who were not his
relatives, of men and women and children, of animals, of ships and cities, of fights, of lovemaking,
of fears and desires—and the memories fought each
other for possession of his crowded skull, threatening to drive his own memories (and thus his own
character) from his head. And as Elric writhed upon
the ground, clutching at his ears, he spoke a word
over and over again in an effort to cling to his own
identity.

'Elric. Elric. Elric.'

And gradually, by an effort which he had experi-
enced only once before when he had summoned
Arioch to the plane of the Earth, he managed to ex-
tinguish all those alien memories and assert his own
until, shaken and feeble, he lowered his hands from
his ears and no longer shouted his own name. And
then he stood up and looked about him.

More than two thirds of his men were dead, blind
or otherwise. The big bosun was dead, his eyes wide
and staring, his lips frozen in a scream, his right eye-
socket raw and bleeding from where he had tried to
drag his eye from it. All the corpses lay in unnatural
positions, all had their eyes open (if they had eyes)
and many bore the marks of self-mutilation, while
others had vomited and others had dashed their
brains against the wall. Dyvim Tvar was alive, but
curled up in a corner, mumbling to himself and Elric
thought he might be mad. Some of the other survivors were, indeed, mad, but they were quiet, they af-
forded no danger. Only five, including Elric, seemed
to have resisted the alien memories and retained
their own sanity. It seemed to Elric, as he stumbled
from corpse to corpse, that most of the men had had
their hearts fail.

'Dyvim Tvar?' Elric put his hand on his friend's shoulder. 'Dyvim Tvar?'

Dyvim Tvar took his head from his arm and looked into Elric's eyes. In Dyvim Tvar's own eyes was the experience of a score of millennia and there was irony there, too. 'I live, Elric.'

'Few of us live now.'

A little later they left the warehouse, no longer needing to fear the mirror, and found that all the streets were full of the dead who had received the mirror's memories. Stiff bodies reached out hands to them. Dead lips formed silent pleas for help. Elric tried not to look at them as he pressed through them, but his desire for vengeance upon his cousin was even stronger now.

They reached the house. The door was open and the ground floor was crammed with corpses. There was no sign of Prince Yyrkoon.

Elric and Dyvim Tvar led the few Imrryrians who were still sane up the steps, past more imploring corpses, until they reached the top floor of the house.

And here they found Cymoril.

She was lying upon a couch and she was naked. There were runes painted on her flesh and the runes were, in themselves, obscene. Her eyelids were heavy and she did not at first recognise them. Elric rushed to her side and cradled her body in his arms. The body was oddly cold.

'He—he makes me—sleep . . .' said Cymoril. 'A sorcerous sleep—from which—only he can wake me . . .' She gave a great yawn. 'I have stayed awake —this long—by an effort of—will—for Elric comes . . .'

'Elric is here,' said her lover, softly. 'I am Elric, Cymoril.'

'Elric?' She relaxed in his arms. 'You—you must

find Yyrkoon—for only he can wake me . . .'

'Where has he gone?' Elric's face had hardened. His crimson eyes were fierce. 'Where?'

'To find the two black swords—the runeswords—of—our ancestors—Mournblade . . .'

'And Stormbringer,' said Elric grimly. 'Those swords are cursed. But where has he gone, Cymoril? How has he escaped us?'

'Through—through—through the—Shade Gate—he conjured it—he made the most fearful pacts with demons to go through . . . The—other—room . . .'

Now Cymoril slept, but there seemed to be a certain peace on her face.

Elric watched as Dyvim Tvar crossed the room, sword in hand, and flung the door open. A dreadful stench came from the next room, which was in darkness. Something flickered on the far side.

'Aye—that's sorcery, right enough,' said Elric. 'And Yyrkoon has thwarted me. He conjured the Shade Gate and passed through it into some netherworld. Which one, I'll never know, for there is an infinity of them. Oh, Arioch, I would give much to follow my cousin!'

'Then follow him you shall,' said a sweet, sardonic voice in Elric's head.

At first the albino thought it was a vestige of a memory still fighting for possession of his head, but then he knew that Arioch spoke to him.

'Dismiss your followers that I may speak with thee,' said Arioch.

Elric hesitated. He wished to be alone—but not with Arioch. He wished to be with Cymoril, for Cymoril was making him weep. Tears already flowed from his crimson eyes.

'What I have to say could result in Cymoril being restored to her normal state,' said the voice. *'And, moreover, it will help you defeat Yyrkoon and be re-*

venged upon him. Indeed, it could make you the most powerful mortal there has ever been.'

Elric looked up at Dyvim Tvar. 'Would you and your men leave me alone for a few moments?'

'Of course.' Dyvim Tvar led his men away and shut the door behind him.

Arioch stood leaning against the same door. Again he had assumed the shape and poise of a handsome youth. His smile was friendly and open and only the ancient eyes belied his appearance.

'It is time to seek the black swords yourself, Elric,' said Arioch. 'Lest Yyrkoon reach them first. I warn you of this—with the runeblades Yyrkoon will be so powerful he will be able to destroy half the world without thinking of it. That is why your cousin risks the dangers of the world beyond the Shade Gate. If Yyrkoon possesses those swords before you find them, it will mean the end of you, of Cymoril, of the Young Kingdoms and, quite possibly, the destruction of Melniboné, too. I will help you enter the netherworld to seek for the twin runeswords.'

Elric said musingly: 'I have often been warned of the dangers of seeking the swords—and the worse dangers of owning them. I think I must consider another plan, my lord Arioch.'

'There is no other plan. Yyrkoon desires the swords if you do not. With Mournblade in one hand and Stormbringer in the other, he will be invincible, for the swords give their user power. Immense power.' Arioch paused.

'You must do as I say. It is to your advantage.'

'And to yours, Lord Arioch?'

'Aye—to mine. I am not entirely selfless.'

Elric shook his head. 'I am confused. There has been too much of the supernatural about this affair. I suspect the gods of manipulating us . . .'

'The gods serve only those who are willing to

serve them. And the gods serve destiny, also.'

'I like it not. To stop Yyrkoon is one thing, to assume his ambitions and take the swords myself—that is another thing.'

'It is your destiny.'

'Cannot I change my destiny?'

Arioch shook his head. 'No more than can I.'

Elric stroked sleeping Cymoril's hair. 'I love her. She is all I desire.'

'You shall not wake her if Yyrkoon finds the blades before you do.'

'And how shall I find the blades?'

'Enter the Shade Gate—I have kept it open, though Yyrkoon thinks it closed—then you must seek the Tunnel Under the Marsh which leads to the Pulsing Cavern. In that chamber the runeswords are kept. They have been kept there ever since your ancestors relinquished them . . .'

'Why were they relinquished.'

'Your ancestors lacked courage.'

'Courage to face what?'

'Themselves.'

'You are cryptic, my lord Arioch.'

'That is the way of the Lords of the Higher Worlds. Hurry. Even I cannot keep the Shade Gate open long.'

'Very well. I will go.'

And Arioch vanished immediately.

Elric called in a hoarse, cracking voice for Dyvim Tvar. Dyvim Tvar entered at once.

'Elric? What has happened in here? Is it Cymoril? You look . . .'

'I am going to follow Yyrkoon—alone, Dyvim Tvar. You must make your way back to Melniboné with those of our men who remain. Take Cymoril with you. If I do not return in reasonable time, you must declare her empress. If she still sleeps, then you must rule as regent until she wakes.'

Dyvim Tvar said softly: 'Do you know what you do, Elric?'

Elric shook his head.

'No, Dyvim Tvar, I do not.'

He got to his feet and staggered towards the other room where the Shade Gate waited for him.

BOOK THREE

And now there is no turning back at all. Elric's destiny has been forged and fixed as surely as the hellswords were forged and fixed aeons before. Was there ever a point where he might have turned off this road to despair, damnation and destruction? Or has he been doomed since before his birth? Doomed through a thousand incarnations to know little else but sadness and struggle, loneliness and remorse—eternally the champion of some unknown cause?

BOOK THREE

1

Through the Shade Gate

AND ELRIC STEPPED into a shadow and found himself in a world of shadows. He turned, but the shadow through which he had entered now faded and was gone. Old Aubec's sword was in Elric's hand, the black helm and the black armour were upon his body and only these were familiar, for the land was dark and gloomy as if contained in a vast cave whose walls, though invisible, were oppressive and tangible. And Elric regretted the hysteria, the weariness of brain, which had given him the impulse to obey his patron demon Arioch and plunge through the Shade Gate. But regret was useless now, so he forgot it.

Yyrkoon was nowhere to be seen. Either Elric's cousin had had a steed awaiting him or else, more likely, he had entered this world at a slightly different angle (for all the planes were said to turn about each other) and was thus either nearer or farther from their mutual goal. The air was rich with brine—so rich that Elric's nostrils felt as if they had been packed with salt—it was almost like walking under water and just being able to breathe the water itself. Perhaps this explained why it was so difficult to see any great distance in any direction, why there were so many shadows, why the sky was like a veil which hid the roof of a cavern. Elric sheathed his sword, there being no evident danger present at that moment, and turned slowly, trying to get some kind of bearing.

It was possible that there were jagged mountains in what he judged the east, and perhaps a forest to the west. Without sun, or stars, or moon, it was hard to gauge distance or direction. He stood on a rocky plain over which whistled a cold and sluggish wind, which tugged at his cloak as if it wished to possess it. There were a few stunted, leafless trees standing in a clump about a hundred paces away. It was all that relieved the bleak plain, save for a large, shapeless slab of rock which stood a fair way beyond the trees. It was a world which seemed to have been drained of all life, where Law and Chaos had once battled and, in their conflict, destroyed all. Were there many planes such as this one? Elric wondered. And for a moment he was filled with a dreadful presentiment concerning the fate of his own rich world. He shook this mood off at once and began to walk towards the trees and the rock beyond.

He reached the trees and passed them, and the touch of his cloak on a branch broke the brittle thing which turned almost at once to ash which was scattered on the wind. Elric drew the cloak closer about his body.

As he approached the rock he became conscious of a sound which seemed to emanate from it. He slowed his pace and put his hand upon the pommel of his sword.

The noise continued—a small, rhythmic noise. Through the gloom Elric peered carefully at the rock, trying to locate the source of the sound.

And then the noise stopped and was replaced by

another—a soft scuffle, a padding footfall, and
then silence. Elric took a pace backward and drew
Aubec's sword. The first sound had been that of a
man sleeping. The second sound was that of a man
waking and preparing himself either for attack or to
defend himself.

Elric said: 'I am Elric of Melniboné. I am a
stranger here.'

And an arrow slid past his helm almost at the
same moment as a bowstring sounded. Elric flung
himself to one side and sought about for cover, but
there was no cover save the rock behind which the
archer hid.

And now a voice came from behind the rock. It
was a firm, rather bleak voice. It said:

'That was not meant to harm you but to display
my skill in case you considered harming me. I have
had my fill of demons in this world and you look
like the most dangerous demon of all, Whiteface.'

'I am mortal,' said Elric, straightening up and deciding that if he must die it would be best to die with
some sort of dignity.

'You spoke of Melniboné. I have heard of the
place. An isle of demons.'

'Then you have not heard enough of Melniboné. I
am mortal as are all my folk. Only the ignorant
think us demons.'

'I am not ignorant, my friend. I am a Warrior
Priest of Phum, born to that caste and the inheritor
of all its knowledge and, until recently, the Lords of
Chaos themselves were my patrons. Then I refused
to serve them longer and was exiled to this plane by
them. Perhaps the same fate befell you, for the folk
of Melniboné serve Chaos do they not?'

'Aye. And I know of Phum—it lies in the unmapped East—beyond the Weeping Waste, beyond
the Sighing Desert, beyond even Elwher. It is one of
the oldest of the Young Kingdoms.'

'All that is so—though I dispute that the East is unmapped, save by the savages of the West. So you are, indeed, to share my exile, it seems.'

'I am not exiled. I am upon a quest. When the quest is done, I shall return to my own world.'

'Return, say you? That interests me, my pale friend. I had thought return impossible.'

'Perhaps it is and I have been tricked. And if your own powers have not found you a way to another plane, perhaps mine will not save me either.'

'Powers? I have none since I relinquished my servitude to Chaos. Well, friend, do you intend to fight me?'

'There is only one upon this plane I would fight and it is not you, Warrior Priest of Phum.' Elric sheathed his sword and at the same moment the speaker rose from behind the rock, replacing a scarlet-fletched arrow in a scarlet quiver.

'I am Rackhir,' said the man. 'Called the Red Archer for, as you see, I affect scarlet dress. It is a habit of the Warrior Priests of Phum to choose but a single colour to wear. It is the only loyalty to tradition I still possess.' He had on a scarlet jerkin, scarlet breeks, scarlet shoes and a scarlet cap with a scarlet feather in it. His bow was scarlet and the pommel of his sword glowed ruby-red. His face, which was aquiline and gaunt, as if carved from fleshless bone, was weather-beaten, and that was brown. He was tall and he was thin, but muscles rippled on his arms and torso. There was irony in his eyes and something of a smile upon his thin lips, though the face showed that it had been through much experience, little of it pleasant.

'An odd place to choose for a quest,' said the Red Archer, standing with hands on hips and looking Elric up and down. 'But I'll strike a bargain with you if you're interested.'

'If the bargain suits me, archer, I'll agree to it, for

you seem to know more of this world than do I.'

'Well—you must find something here and then leave, whereas I have nothing at all to do here and wish to leave. If I help you in your quest, will you take me with you when you return to our own plane?'

'That seems a fair bargain, but I cannot promise what I have no power to give. I will say only this—if it is possible for me to take you back with me to our own plane, either before or after I have finished my quest, I will do it.'

'That is reasonable,' said Rackhir the Red Archer. 'Now—tell me what you seek.'

'I seek two swords, forged millennia ago by immortals, used by my ancestors but then relinquished by them and placed upon this plane. The swords are large and heavy and black and they have cryptic runes carved into their blades. I was told that I would find them in the Pulsing Cavern which is reached through the Tunnel Under the Marsh. Have you heard of either of these places?'

'I have not. Nor have I heard of the two black swords.' Rackhir rubbed his bony chin. 'Though I remember reading something in one of the Books of Phum and what I read disturbed me . . .'

'The swords are legendary. Many books make some small reference to them—almost always mysterious. There is said to be one tome which records the history of the swords and all who have used them—and all who will use them in the future—a timeless book which contains all time. Some call it the Chronicle of the Black Sword and in it, it is said, men may read their whole destinies.'

'I know nothing of that, either. It is not one of the Books of Phum. I fear, Comrade Elric, that we shall have to venture to the City of Ameeron and ask your questions of the inhabitants there.'

'There is a city upon this plane?'

'Aye—a city. I stayed but a short time in it, preferring the wilderness. But with a friend, it might be possible to bear the place a little longer.'

'Why is Ameeron unsuited to your taste?'

'Its citizens are not happy. Indeed, they are a most depressed and depressing group, for they are all, you see, exiles or refugees or travelers between the worlds who lost their way and never found it again. No one lives in Ameeron by choice.'

'A veritable City of the Damned.'

'As the poet might remark, aye.' Rackhir offered Elric a sardonic wink. 'But I sometimes think all cities are that.'

'What is the nature of this plane where are, as far as I can tell, no planets, no moon, no sun. It has something of the air of a great cavern.'

'There is, indeed, a theory that it is a sphere buried in an infinity of rock. Others say that it lies in the future of our own Earth—a future where the universe has died. I heard a thousand theories during the short space of time I spend in the City of Ameeron. All, it seemed to me, were of equal value. All, it seemed to me, could be correct. Why not? There are some who believe that everything is a Lie. Conversely, everything could be the Truth.'

It was Elric's turn to remark ironically: 'You are a philosopher, then, as well as an archer, friend Rackhir of Phum?'

Rackhir laughed. 'If you like! It is such thinking that weakened my loyalty to Chaos and led me to this pass. I have heard that there is a city called Tanelorn which may sometimes be found on the shifting shores of the Sighing Desert. If I ever return to our own world, Comrade Elric, I shall seek that city, for I have heard that peace may be found there—that such debates as the nature of Truth are considered meaningless. That men are content merely to exist in Tanelorn.'

'I envy those who dwell in Tanelorn,' said Elric.

Rackhir sniffed. 'Aye. But it would probably prove a disappointment, if found. Legends are best left as legends and attempts to make them real are rarely successful. Come—yonder lies Ameeron and that, sad to say, is more typical of most cities one comes across—on any plane.'

The two tall men, both outcasts in their different ways, began to trudge through the gloom of that desolate wasteland.

2

In the City of Ameeron

THE CITY OF AMEERON came in sight and Elric had never seen such a place before. Ameeron made Dhoz-Kam seem like the cleanest and most well-run settlement there could be. The city lay below the plain of rocks, in a shallow valley over which hung perpetual smoke: a filthy, tattered cloak meant to hide the place from the sight of men and gods.

The buildings were mostly in a state of semi-ruin or else were wholly ruined and shacks and tents erected in their place. The mixture of architectural styles—some familiar, some most alien—was such that Elric was hard put to see one building which resembled another. There were shanties and castles, cottages, towers and forts, plain, square villas and wooden huts heavy with carved ornamentation. Others seemed merely piles of rock with a jagged opening at one end for a door. But none looked well—could not have looked well in that landscape under that perpetually gloomy sky.

Here and there red fires sputtered, adding to the smoke, and the smell as Elric and Rackhir reached the outskirts was rich with a great variety of stinks.

'Arrogance, rather than pride, is the paramount quality of most of Ameeron's residents,' said Rackhir, wrinkling his hawklike nose. 'Where they have any qualities of character left at all.'

Elric trudged through filth. Shadows scuttled amongst the close-packed buildings. 'Is there an inn, perhaps, where we can enquire after the Tunnel Under the Marsh and its whereabouts?'

'No inn. By and large the inhabitants keep themselves to themselves . . .'

'A city square where folk meet?'

'This city has no centre. Each resident or group of residents built their own dwelling where they felt like it, or where there was space, and they come from all planes and all ages, thus the confusion, the decay and the oldness of many of the places. Thus the filth, the hopelessness, the decadence of the majority.'

'How do they live?'

'They live off each other, by and large. They trade with demons who occasionally visit Ameeron from time to time . . .'

'Demons?'

'Aye. And the bravest hunt the rats which dwell in the caverns below the city.'

'What demons are these?'

'Just creatures, mainly minor minions of Chaos, who want something that the Ameeronese can supply—a stolen soul or two, a baby, perhaps (though few are born here)—you can imagine what else, if you've knowledge of what demons normally demand from sorcerers.'

'Aye. I can imagine. So Chaos can come and go on this plane as it pleases.'

'I'm not sure it's quite as easy. But it is certainly easier for the demons to travel back and forth here than it would be for them to travel back and forth in our plane.'

'Have you seen any of these demons?'

'Aye. The usual bestial sort. Coarse, stupid and powerful—many of them were once human before electing to bargain with Chaos. Now they are mentally and physically warped into foul, demon shapes.'

Elric found Rackhir's words not to his taste. 'Is that ever the fate of those who bargain with Chaos?' he said.

'You should know, if you come from Melniboné. I know that in Phum it is rarely the case. But it seems that the higher the stakes the subtler are the changes a man undergoes when Chaos agrees to trade with him.'

Elric sighed. 'Where shall we enquire of our Tunnel Under the Marsh?'

'There was an old man . . .' Rackhir began, and then a grunt behind him made him pause.

Another grunt.

A face with tusks in it emerged from a patch of darkness formed by a fallen slab of masonry. The face grunted again.

'Who are you?' said Elric, his sword-hand ready.

'Pig,' said the face with tusks in it. Elric was not certain whether he was being insulted or whether the creature was describing himself.

'Pig.'

Two more faces with tusks in them came out of the patch of darkness. 'Pig,' said one.

'Pig,' said another.

'Snake,' said a voice behind Elric and Rackhir. Elric turned while Rackhir continued to watch the pigs. A tall youth stood there. Where his head would have been sprouted the bodies of about fifteen good-sized snakes. The head of each snake glared at Elric. The tongues flickered and they all opened their mouths at exactly the same moment to say again:

'Snake.'

'Thing,' said another voice. Elric glanced in that direction, gasped, drew his sword and felt nausea sweep through him.

Then Pigs, Snake and Thing were upon them.

Rackhir took one Pig before it could move three paces. His bow was off his back and strung and a red-fletched arrow nocked and shot, all in a second. He had time to shoot one more Pig and then drop his bow to draw his sword. Back to back he and Elric prepared to defend themselves against the demons' attack. Snake was bad enough, with its fifteen darting heads hissing and snapping with teeth which dripped venom, but Thing kept changing its form—first an arm would emerge, then a face would appear from the shapeless, heaving flesh which shuffled implacably closer.

'Thing!' it shouted. Two swords slashed at Elric who was dealing with the last Pig and missed his stroke so that instead of running the Pig through the heart, he took him in a lung. Pig staggered backward and slumped to the ground in a pool of muck. He crawled for a moment, but then collapsed. Thing had produced a spear and Elric barely managed to deflect the cast with the flat of his sword. Now Rackhir was engaged with Snake and the two demons closed on the men, eager to make a finish of them. Half the heads of Snake lay writhing on the ground and Elric had managed to slice one hand off Thing, but the demon still seemed to have three other hands ready. It seemed to be created not from one creature but from several. Elric wondered if, through his bargaining with Arioch, this would ultimately be his fate, to be turned into a demon—a formless monster. But wasn't he already something of a monster? Didn't folk already mistake him for a demon?

These thoughts gave him strength. He yelled as he fought. 'Elric!'

And: 'Thing!' replied his adversary, also eager to assert what he regarded as the essence of his being.

Another hand flew off as Aubec's sword bit into it. Another javelin jabbed out and was knocked aside; another sword appeared and came down on Elric's helm with a force which dazed him and sent him reeling back against Rackhir who missed his thrust at Snake and was almost bitten by four of the heads. Elric chopped at the arm and the tentacle which held the sword and saw them part from the body but then become reabsorbed again. The nausea returned. Elric thrust his sword into the mass and the mass screamed: 'Thing! Thing! Thing!'

Elric thrust again and four swords and two spears waved and clashed and tried to deflect Aubec's blade.

'Thing!'

'This is Yyrkoon's work,' said Elric, 'without a doubt. He has heard that I have followed him and seeks to stop us with his demon allies.' He gritted his teeth and spoke through them. 'Unless one of these is Yyrkoon himself! Are you my cousin Yyrkoon, Thing?'

'Thing . . .' The voice was almost pathetic. The weapons waved and clashed but they no longer darted so fiercely at Elric.

'Or are you some other old, familiar friend?'

'Thing . . .'

Elric stabbed again and again into the mass. Thick, reeking blood spurted and fell upon his armour. Elric could not understand why it had become so easy to take the attack to the demon.

'Now!' shouted a voice from above Elric's head. 'Quickly!'

Elric glanced up and saw a red face, a white

beard, a waving arm. 'Don't look at me you fool! Now—strike!'

And Elric put his two hands above his sword hilt and drove the blade deep into the shapeless creature which moaned and wept and said in a small whisper 'Frank . . .' before it died.

Rackhir thrust at the same moment and his blade went under the remaining snake heads and plunged into the chest and thence into the heart of the youth-body and his demon died, too.

The white-haired man came clambering down from the ruined archway on which he had been perched. He was laughing. 'Niun's sorcery still has some effect, even here, eh? I heard the tall one call his demon friends and instruct them to set upon you. It did not seem fair to me that five should attack two—so I sat upon that wall and I drew the many-armed demon's strength out of it. I still can. I still can. And now I have his strength (or a fair part of it) and feel considerably better than I have done for many a moon (if such a thing exists).'

'It said "Frank",' said Elric frowning. 'Was that a name, do you think? Its name before?'

'Perhaps,' said old Niun, 'perhaps. Poor creature. But still, it is dead now. You are not of Ameeron, you two—though I've seen you here before, red one.'

'And I've seen you,' said Rackhir with a smile. He wiped Snake's blood from his blade, using one of Snake's heads for the purpose. 'You are Niun Who Knew All.'

'Aye. Who Knew All but who now knows very little. Soon it will be over, when I have forgotten everything. Then I may return from this awful exile. It is the pact I made with Orland of the Staff. I was a fool who wished to know everything and my curiosity led me into an adventure concerning this Orland. Orland showed me the error of my ways and sent me here to forget. Sadly, as you noticed, I still remember some of my powers and my knowledge from time to time. I know you seek the Black Swords. I know you are Elric of Melniboné. I know what will become of you.'

'You know my destiny?' said Elric eagerly. 'Tell me what it is Niun Who Knew All!'

Niun opened his mouth as if to speak but then firmly shut it again. 'No,' he said. 'I have forgotten.'

'No!' Elric made as if to seize the old man. 'No! You remember! I can see that you remember!'

'I have forgotten.' Niun lowered his head.

Rackhir took hold of Elric's arm. 'He has forgotten, Elric.'

Elric nodded. 'Very well.' Then he said, 'But have you remembered where lies the Tunnel Under the Marsh?'

'Yes. It is only a short distance from Ameeron, the Marsh itself. You go that way. Then you look for a monument in the shape of an eagle carved in black marble. At the base of the monument is the entrance to the tunnel.' Niun repeated this information parrot-fashion and when he looked up his face was clearer. 'What did I just tell you?'

Elric said: 'You gave us instructions on how to reach the entrance to the Tunnel Under the Marsh.'

'Did I?' Niun clapped his old hands. 'Splendid. I have forgotten that now, too. Who are you?'

'We are best forgotten,' said Rackhir with a gentle smile. 'Farewell, Niun and thanks.'

'Thanks for what?'

'Both for remembering and for forgetting.'

They walked on through the miserable City of Ameeron, away from the happy old sorcerer, sighting the odd face staring at them from a doorway or a window, doing their best to breathe as little of the foul air as possible.

'I think perhaps that I envy Niun alone of all the inhabitants of this desolate place,' said Rackhir.

'I pity him,' said Elric.

'Why so?'

'It occurs to me that when he has forgotten everything, he may well forget that he is allowed to leave Ameeron.'

Rackhir laughed and slapped the albino upon his black armoured back. 'You are a gloomy comrade, friend Elric. Are all your thoughts so hopeless?'

'They tend in that direction, I fear,' said Elric with a shadow of a smile.

3

The Tunnel Under the Marsh

AND ON THEY travelled through that sad and murky world until at last they came to the marsh.

The marsh was black. Black spiky vegetation grew in clumps here and there upon it. It was cold and it was dank; a dark mist swirled close to the surface and through the mist sometimes darted low shapes. From the mist rose a solid black object which could only be the monument described by Niun.

'The monument,' said Rackhir, stopping and leaning on his bow. 'It's well out into the marsh and there's no evident pathway leading to it. Is this a problem, do you think, Comrade Elric?'

Elric waded cautiously into the edge of the marsh. He felt the cold ooze drag at his feet. He stepped back with some difficulty.

'There must be a path,' said Rackhir, fingering his bony nose. 'Else how would your cousin cross?'

Elric looked over his shoulder at the Red Archer and he shrugged. 'Who knows? He could be travelling with sorcerous companions who have no difficulty where marshes are concerned.'

Suddenly Elric found himself sitting down upon the damp rock. The stink of brine from the marsh seemed for a moment to have overwhelmed him. He was feeling weak. The effectiveness of his drugs, last taken just as he stepped through the Shade Gate, was beginning to fade.

Rackhir came and stood by the albino. He smiled with a certain amount of bantering sympathy. 'Well, Sir Sorcerer, cannot you summon similar aid?'

Elric shook his head. 'I know little that is practical concerning the raising of small demons. Yyrkoon has all his grimoires, his favourite spells, his introductions to the demon worlds. We shall have to find a path of the ordinary kind if we wish to reach yonder monument, Warrior Priest of Phum.'

The Warrior Priest of Phum drew a red kerchief from within his tunic and blew his nose for some time. When he had finished he put down a hand, helped Elric to his feet, and began to walk along the rim of the marsh, keeping the black monument ever in sight.

It was some time later that they found a path at last and it was not a natural path but a slab of black marble extending out into the gloom of the mire, slippery to the feet and itself covered with a film of ooze.

'I would almost suspect this of being a false path—a lure to take us to our death,' said Rackhir as he and Elric stood and looked at the long slab, 'but what have we to lose now?'

'Come,' said Elric, setting foot on the slab and beginning to make his cautious way along it. In his hand he now held a torch of sorts, a bundle of sputtering reeds which gave off an unpleasant yellow light and a considerable amount of greenish smoke, but it was better than nothing.

Rackhir, testing each footstep with his unstrung bow-stave, followed behind, whistling a small, complicated tune as he went along. Another of his race would have recognised the tune as the *Song of the Son of the Hero of the High Hell who is about to Sacrifice his Life,* a popular melody in Phum, particularly amongst the caste of the Warrior Priest.

Elric found the tune irritating and distracting, but he said nothing, for he concentrated every fragment of his attention on keeping his balance upon the slippery surface of the slab, which now appeared to rock slightly, as if it floated on the surface of the marsh.

And now they were halfway to the monument whose shape could be clearly distinguished: A great eagle with spread wings and a savage beak and claws extended for the kill. An eagle in the same black marble as the slab on which they tried to keep their balance. And Elric was reminded of a tomb. Had some ancient hero been buried here? Or had the tomb been built to house the Black Swords—imprison them so that they might never enter the world of men again and steal men's souls?

The slab rocked more violently. Elric tried to remain upright but swayed first on one foot and then the other, the brand waving crazily. Both feet slid from under him and he went flying into the marsh and was instantly buried up to his knees.

He began to sink.

Somehow he had managed to keep his grip on the brand and by its light he could see the red-clad archer peering forward.

'Elric?'

'I'm here, Rackhir.'

'You're sinking?'

'The marsh seems intent on swallowing me, aye.'

'Can you lie flat?'

'I can lie forward, but my legs are trapped.' Elric tried to move his body in the ooze which pressed against it. Something rushed past him in front of his face, giving voice to a kind of muted gibbering. Elric did his best to control the fear which welled up in him. 'I think you must give me up, friend Rackhir.'

'What? And lose my means of getting out of this world? You must think me more selfless than I am, Comrade Elric. Here . . .' Rackhir carefully lowered himself to the slab and reached out his arm towards Elric. Both men were now covered in clinging slime; both shivered with cold. Rackhir stretched and stretched and Elric leaned forward as far as he could and tried to reach the hand, but it was impossible. And every second dragged him deeper into the stinking filth of the marsh.

Then Rackhir took up his bow-stave and pushed that out.

'Grab the bow, Elric. Can you?'

Leaning forward and stretching every bone and muscle in his body, Elric just managed to get a grip on the bow-stave.

'Now, I must—Ah!' Rackhir, pulling at the bow, found his own feet slipping and the slab beginning to rock quite wildly. He flung out one arm to grab the far lip of the slab and with his other hand kept a grip on the bow, 'Hurry, Elric! Hurry!'

Elric began painfully to pull himself from the ooze. The slab still rocked crazily and Rackhir's hawklike face was almost as pale as Elric's own as he desperately strove to keep his hold on both slab and bow. And then Elric, all soaked in mire, managed to reach the slab and crawl onto it, the brand still sputtering in his hand, and lie there gasping and gasping and gasping.

Rackhir, too, was short of breath, but he laughed. 'What a fish I've caught!' he said. 'The biggest yet, I'd wager!'

'I am grateful to you, Rackhir the Red Archer. I am grateful, Warrior Priest of Phum. I owe you my life,' said Elric after a while. 'And I swear that whether I'm successful in my quest or not I'll use all my powers to see you through the Shade Gate and back into the world from which we have both come.'

Rackhir said quietly: 'You are a man, Elric of Melniboné. That is why I saved you. There are few men in any world.' He shrugged and grinned. 'Now I suggest we continue towards yonder monument on our knees. Undignified it might be, but safer it is also. And it is but a short way to crawl.'

Elric agreed.

Not much more time had passed in that timeless darkness before they had reached a little moss-grown island on which stood the Monument of the Eagle, huge and heavy and towering above them into the greater gloom which was either the sky or the roof of the cavern. And at the base of the plinth they saw a low doorway. And the doorway was open.

'A trap?' mused Rackhir.

'Or does Yyrkoon assume us perished in Ameeron?' said Elric, wiping himself free of slime as best he could. He sighed. 'Let's enter and be done with it.'

And so they entered.

They found themselves in a small room. Elric cast the faint light of a brand about the place and saw another doorway. The rest of the room was featureless—each wall made of the same faintly glistening black marble. The room was filled with silence.

Neither man spoke. Both walked unfalteringly towards the next doorway and, when they found steps, began to descend the steps, which wound down and down into total darkness.

For a long time they descended, still without speaking, until eventually they reached the bottom and saw before them the entrance to a narrow tunnel which was irregularly shaped so that it seemed more the work of nature than of some intelligence. Moisture dripped from the roof of the tunnel and fell with the regularity of heartbeats to the floor, seeming to echo a deeper sound, far, far away, emanating from somewhere in the tunnel itself.

Elric heard Rackhir clear his throat.

'This is without doubt a tunnel,' said the Red Archer, 'and it, unquestionably leads under the marsh.'

Elric felt that Rackhir shared his reluctance to enter the tunnel. He stood with the guttering brand held high, listening to the sound of the drops falling to the floor of the tunnel, trying to recognise that other sound which came so faintly from the depths.

And then he forced himself forward, almost running into the tunnel, his ears filled with a sudden roaring which might have come from within his head or from some other source in the tunnel. He heard Rackhir's footfalls behind him. He drew his sword, the sword of the dead hero Aubec, and he heard the hissing of his own breath echo from the walls of the tunnel which was now alive with sounds of every sort.

Elric shuddered, but he did not pause.

The tunnel was warm. The floor felt spongy beneath his feet, the smell of brine persisted. And now he could see that the walls of the tunnel were smoother, that they seemed to shiver with quick, regular movement. He heard Rackhir gasp behind him as the archer, too, noted the peculiar nature of the tunnel.

'It's like flesh,' murmured the Warrior Priest of Phum. 'Like flesh.'

Elric could not bring himself to reply. All his attention was required to force himself forward. He was consumed by terror. His whole body shook. He sweated and his legs threatened to buckle under him. His grip was so weak that he could barely keep his sword from falling to the floor. And there were hints of something in his memory, something which his brain refused to consider. Had he been here before? His trembling increased. His stomach turned. But he still stumbled on, the brand held before him.

And now the soft, steady thrumming sound grew louder and he saw ahead a small, almost circular aperture at the very end of the tunnel. He stopped, swaying.

'The tunnel ends,' whispered Rackhir. 'There is no way through.'

The small aperture was pulsing with a swift, strong beat.

'The Pulsing Cavern,' Elric whispered. 'That is what we should find at the end of the Tunnel Under the Marsh. That must be the entrance, Rackhir.'

'It is too small for a man to enter, Elric,' said Rackhir reasonably.

'No . . .'

Elric stumbled forward until he stood close to the opening. He sheathed his sword. He handed the brand to Rackhir and then, before the Warrior Priest of Phum could stop him, he had flung himself headfirst through the gap, wriggling his body through—and the walls of the aperture parted for him and then closed behind him, leaving Rackhir on the other side.

Elric got slowly to his feet. A faint, pinkish light now came from the walls and ahead of him was another entrance, slightly larger than the other through which he had just come. The air was warm and thick and salty. It almost stifled him. His head throbbed and his body ached and he could barely act or think, save to force himself onward. On faltering legs he flung himself towards the next entrance as the great, muffled pulsing sounded louder and louder in his ears.

'Elric!'

Rackhir stood behind him, pale and sweating. He had abandoned the brand and followed Elric through.

Elric licked dry lips and tried to speak.

Rackhir came closer.

Elric said thickly: 'Rackhir. You should not be here.'

'I said I would help.'

'Aye, but . . .'

'Then help I shall.'

Elric had no strength for arguing, so he nodded and with his hands forced back the soft walls of the second aperture and saw that it led into a cavern whose round wall quivered to a steady pulsing. And in the centre of the cavern, hanging in the air without any support at all were two swords. Two identical swords, huge and fine and black.

And standing beneath the swords, his expression gloating and greedy, stood Prince Yyrkoon of Melniboné, reaching up for them, his lips moving but no words escaping from him. And Elric himself was able to voice but one word as he climbed through and stood upon that shuddering floor. 'No,' he said.

Yyrkoon heard the word. He turned with terror in his face. He snarled when he saw Elric and then he, too, voiced a word which was at once a scream of outrage.

'No!'

With an effort Elric dragged Aubec's blade from its scabbard. But it seemed too heavy to hold upright, it tugged his arm so that it rested on the floor, his arm hanging straight at his side. Elric drew deep breaths of heavy air into his lungs. His vision was dimming. Yyrkoon had become a shadow. Only the two black swords, standing still and cool in the very centre of the circular chamber, were in focus. Elric sensed Rackhir enter the chamber and stand beside him.

'Yyrkoon,' said Elric at last, 'those swords are mine.'

Yyrkoon smiled and reached up towards the blades. A peculiar moaning sound seemed to issue from them. A faint, black radiance seemed to emanate from them. Elric saw the runes carved into them and he was afraid.

Rackhir fitted an arrow to his bow. He drew the string back to his shoulder, sighting along the arrow at Prince Yyrkoon. 'If he must die, Elric, tell me.'

'Slay him,' said Elric.

And Rackhir released the string.

But the arrow moved very slowly through the air and then hung halfway between the archer and his intended target.

Yyrkoon turned, a ghastly grin on his face. 'Mortal weapons are useless here,' he said.

Elric said to Rackhir, 'He must be right. And your life is in danger, Rackhir. Go . . .'

Rackhir gave him a puzzled look. 'No, I must stay here and help you . . .'

Elric shook his head. 'You cannot help, you will only die if you stay. Go.'

Reluctantly the Red Archer unstrung his bow, glanced suspiciously up at the two black swords, then squeezed his way through the doorway and was gone.

'Now, Yyrkoon,' said Elric, letting Aubec's sword fall to the floor. 'We must settle this, you and I.'

4

Two Black Swords

AND THEN THE runeblades Stormbringer and Mournblade were gone from where they had hung so long.

And Stormbringer had settled into Elric's right hand. And Mournblade lay in Prince Yyrkoon's right hand.

And the two men stood on opposite sides of the Pulsing Cavern and regarded first each other and then the swords they held.

The swords were singing. Their voices were faint but could be heard quite plainly. Elric lifted the huge blade easily and turned it this way and that, admiring its alien beauty.

'Stormbringer,' he said.

And then he felt afraid.

It was suddenly as if he had been born again and that this runesword was born with him. It was as if they had never been separate.

'Stormbringer.'

And the sword moaned sweetly and settled even more smoothly into his grasp.

'Stormbringer!' yelled Elric and he leapt at his cousin.

'Stormbringer!'

And he was full of fear—so full of fear. And the fear brought a wild kind of delight—a demonic need to fight and kill his cousin, to sink the blade deep into Yyrkoon's heart. To take vengeance. To spill blood. To send a soul to hell.

And now Prince Yyrkoon's cry could be heard above the thrum of the sword-voices, the drumming of the pulse of the cavern.

'Mournblade!'

And Mournblade came up to meet Stormbringer's blow and turn that blow and thrust back at Elric who swayed aside and brought Stormbringer round and down in a sidestroke which knocked Yyrkoon and Mournblade backward for an instant. But Stormbringer's next thrust was met again. And the next thrust was met. And the next. If the swordsmen were evenly matched, then so were the blades, which seemed possessed of their own wills, though they performed the wills of their wielders.

And the clang of the metal upon metal turned into a wild, metallic song which the swords sang. A joyful song as if they were glad at last to be back to battling, though they battled each other.

And Elric barely saw his cousin, Prince Yyrkoon, at all, save for an occasional flash of his dark, wild face. Elric's attention was given entirely to the two black swords, for it seemed that the swords fought with the life of one of the swordsmen as a prize (or perhaps the lives of both, thought Elric) and that the rivalry between Elric and Yyrkoon was nothing compared with the brotherly rivalry between the swords who seemed full of pleasure at the chance to engage again after many millennia.

And this observation, as he fought—and fought for his soul as well as his life—gave Elric pause to consider his hatred of Yyrkoon.

Kill Yyrkoon he would, but not at the will of another power. Not to give sport to these alien swords.

Mournblade's point darted at his eyes and Stormbringer rose to deflect the thrust once more.

Elric no longer fought his cousin. He fought the will of the two black swords.

Stormbringer dashed for Yyrkoon's momentarily undefended throat. Elric clung to the sword and dragged it back, sparing his cousin's life. Stormbringer whined almost petulantly, like a dog stopped from biting an intruder.

And Elric spoke through clenched teeth. 'I'll not be your puppet, runeblade. If we must be united, let it be upon a proper understanding.'

The sword seemed to hesitate, to drop its guard, and Elric was hard put to defend himself against the whirling attack of Mournblade which, in turn, seemed to sense its advantage.

Elric felt fresh energy pour up his right arm and into his body. This was what the sword could do. With it, he needed no drugs, would never be weak again. In battle he would triumph. At peace, he could rule with pride. When he travelled, it could be alone and without fear. It was as if the sword reminded him of all these things, even as it returned Mournblade's attack.

And what must the sword have in return?

Elric knew. The sword told him, without words of any sort. Stormbringer needed to fight, for that was its reason for existence. Stormbringer needed to kill, for that was its source of energy, the lives and the souls of men, demons—even gods.

And Elric hesitated, even as his cousin gave a huge, cackling yell and dashed at him so that Mournblade glanced off his helm and he was flung backwards and down and saw Yyrkoon gripping his moaning black sword in both hands to plunge the runeblade into Elric's body.

And Elric knew he would do anything to resist
that fate—for his soul to be drawn into Mournblade
and his strength to feed Prince Yyrkoon's strength.
And he rolled aside, very quickly, and got to one
knee and turned and lifted Stormbringer with one
gauntleted hand upon the blade and the other upon
the hilt to take the great blow Prince Yyrkoon
brought upon it. And the two black swords shrieked
as if in pain, and they shivered, and black radiance
poured from them as blood might pour from a man
pierced by many arrows. And Elric was driven, still
on his knees, away from the radiance, gasping and
sighing and peering here and there for sight of
Yyrkoon who had disappeared.

And Elric knew that Stormbringer spoke to him
again. If Elric did not wish to die by Mournblade,
then Elric must accept the bargain which the Black
Sword offered.

'He must not die!' said Elric. 'I will not slay him
to make sport for you!'

And through the black radiance ran Yyrkoon,
snarling and snapping and whirling his runesword.

Again Stormbringer darted through an opening,
and again Elric made the blade pull back and
Yyrkoon was only grazed.

Stormbringer writhed in Elric's hands.

Elric said: 'You shall not be my master.'

And Stormbringer seemed to understand and become quieter, as if reconciled. And Elric laughed,
thinking that he now controlled the runesword and
that from now on the blade would do his bidding.

'We shall disarm Yyrkoon,' said Elric. 'We shall
not kill him.'

Elric rose to his feet.

Stormbringer moved with all the speed of a
needle-thin rapier. It feinted, it parried, it thrust.
Yyrkoon, who had been grinning in triumph,
snarled and staggered back, the grin dropping from

his sullen features.

Stormbringer now worked for Elric. It made the moves that Elric wished to make. Both Yyrkoon and Mournblade seemed disconcerted by this turn of events. Mournblade shouted as if in astonishment at its brother's behaviour. Elric struck at Yyrkoon's sword-arm, pierced cloth—pierced flesh—pierced sinew—pierced bone. Blood came, soaking Yyrkoon's arm and dripping down onto the hilt of the sword. The blood was slippery. It weakened Yyrkoon's grip on his runesword. He took it in both hands, but he was unable to hold it firmly.

Elric, too, took Stormbringer in both hands. Unearthly strength surged through him. With a gigantic blow he dashed Stormbringer against Mournblade where blade met hilt. The runesword few from Yyrkoon's grasp. It sped across the Pulsing Cavern.

Elric smiled. He had defeated his own sword's will and, in turn, had defeated the brother sword.

Mournblade fell against the wall of the Pulsing Cavern and for a moment was still.

A groan then seemed to escape the defeated runesword. A high-pitched shriek filled the Pulsing Cavern. Blackness flooded over the eery pink light and extinguished it.

When the light returned Elric saw that a scabbard lay at his feet. The scabbard was black and of the same alien craftsmanship as the runesword. Elric saw Yyrkoon. The prince was on his knees and he was sobbing, his eyes darting about the Pulsing Cavern seeking Mournblade, looking at Elric with fright as if he knew he must now be slain.

'Mournblade?' Yyrkoon said hopelessly. He knew he was to die.

Mournblade had vanished from the Pulsing Cavern.

'Your sword is gone,' said Elric quietly.

Yyrkoon whimpered and tried to crawl towards the entrance of the cavern. But the entrance had shrunk to the size of a small coin. Yyrkoon wept.

Stormbringer trembled, as if thirsty for Yyrkoon's soul. Elric stooped.

Yyrkoon began to speak rapidly. 'Do not slay me, Elric—not with that runeblade. I will do anything you wish. I will die in any other way.'

Elric said: 'We are victims, cousin, of a conspiracy—a game played by gods, demons and sentient swords. They wish one of us dead. I suspect they wish you dead more than they wish me dead. And that is the reason why I shall not slay you here.' He picked up the scabbard. He forced Stormbringer into it and at once the sword was quiet. Elric took off his old scabbard and looked around for Aubec's sword, but that, too, was gone. He dropped the old scabbard and hooked the new one to his belt. He rested his left hand upon the pommel of Stormbringer and he looked not without sympathy upon the creature that was his cousin.

'You are a worm, Yyrkoon. But is that your fault?'

Yyrkoon gave him a puzzled glance.

'I wonder, if you had all your desire, would you cease to be a worm, cousin?'

Yyrkoon raised himself to his knees. A little hope began to show in his eyes.

Elric smiled and drew a deep breath. 'We shall see,' he said. 'You must agree to wake Cymoril from her sorcerous slumber.'

'You have humbled me, Elric,' said Yyrkoon in a small, pitiful voice. 'I will wake her. Or would . . .'

'Can you not undo your spell?'

'We cannot escape from the Pulsing Cavern. It is past the time . . .'

'What's this?'

'I did not think you would follow me. And then I

thought I would easily finish you. And now it is past the time. One can keep the entrance open for only a little while. It will admit anyone who cares to enter the Pulsing Cavern, but it will let no-one out after the power of the spell dies. I gave much to know that spell.'

'You have given too much for everything,' said Elric. He went to the entrance and peered through. Rackhir waited on the other side. The Red Archer had an anxious expression. Elric said: 'Warrior Priest of Phum, it seems that my cousin and I are trapped in here. The entrance will not part for us.' Elric tested the warm, moist stuff of the wall. It would not open more than a tiny fraction. 'It seems that you can join us or else go back. If you do join us, you share our fate.'

'It is not much of a fate if I go back,' said Rackhir. 'What chances have you?'

'One,' said Elric. 'I can invoke my patron.'

'A Lord of Chaos?' Rackhir made a wry face.

'Exactly,' said Elric. 'I speak of Arioch.'

'Arioch, eh? Well, he does not care for renegades from Phum.'

'What do you choose to do?'

Rackhir stepped forward. Elric stepped back. Through the opening came Rackhir's head, followed by his shoulders, followed by the rest of him. The entrance closed again immediately. Rackhir stood up and untangled the string of his bow from the stave, smoothing it. 'I agreed to share your fate—to gamble all on escaping from this plane,' said the Red Archer. He looked surprised when he saw Yyrkoon. 'Your enemy is still alive?'

'Aye.'

'You are merciful indeed!'

'Perhaps. Or obstinate. I would not slay him merely because some supernatural agency used him as a pawn, to be killed if I should win. The Lords of the higher Worlds do not as yet control me completely—nor will they if I have any power at all to resist them.'

Rackhir grinned. 'I share your view—though I'm not optimistic about its realism. I see you have one of those black swords at your belt. Will that not hack a way through the cavern?'

'No,' said Yyrkoon from his place against the wall. 'Nothing can harm the stuff of the Pulsing Cavern.'

'I'll believe you,' said Elric, 'for I do not intend to draw this new sword of mine often. I must learn how to control it first.'

'So Arioch must be summoned.' Rackhir sighed.

'If that is possible,' said Elric.

'He will doubtless destroy me,' said Rackhir, looking to Elric in the hope that the albino would deny this statement.

Elric looked grave. 'I might be able to strike a bargain with him. It will also test something.'

Elric turned his back on Rackhir and on Yyrkoon. He adjusted his mind. He sent it out through vast spaces and complicated mazes. And he cried:

'Arioch! Arioch! Aid me, Arioch!'

He had a sense of something listening to him.

'Arioch!'

Something shifted in the places where his mind went.

'Arioch . . .'

And Arioch heard him. He knew it was Arioch.

Rackhir gave a horrified yell. Yyrkoon screamed. Elric turned and saw that something disgusting had appeared near the far wall. It was black and it was foul and it slobbered and its shape was intolerably alien. Was this Arioch? How could it be? Arioch was beautiful. But perhaps, thought Elric, this was Arioch's true shape. Upon this plane, in this peculiar cavern, Arioch could not deceive those who looked upon him.

But then the shape had disappeared and a beautiful youth with ancient eyes stood looking at the three mortals.

'You have won the sword, Elric,' said Arioch, ignoring the others. 'I congratulate you. And you have spared your cousin's life. Why so?'

'More than one reason,' said Elric. 'But let us say he must remain alive in order to wake Cymoril.'

Arioch's face bore a little, secret smile for a moment and Elric realised that he had avoided a trap. If he had killed Yyrkoon, Cymoril would never have woken again.

'And what is this little traitor doing with you?' Arioch turned a cold eye on Rackhir who did his best to stare back at the Chaos Lord.

'He is my friend,' said Elric. 'I made a bargain with him. If he aided me to find the Black Sword, then I would take him back with me to our own plane.'

'That is impossible. Rackhir is an exile here. That is his punishment.'

'He comes back with me,' said Elric. And now he unhooked the scabbard holding Stormbringer from his belt and he held the sword out before him. 'Or I do not take the sword with me. Failing that, we all three remain here for eternity.'

'That is not sensible, Elric. Consider your responsibilities.'

'I have considered them. That is my decision.'

Arioch's smooth face had just a tinge of anger. 'You must take the sword. It is your destiny.'

'So you say. But I now know that the sword may only be borne by me. You cannot bear it, Arioch, or you would. Only I—or another mortal like me—can take it from the Pulsing Cavern. Is that not so?'

'You are clever, Elric of Melniboné.' Arioch spoke with sardonic admiration. 'And you are a fitting ser-

vant of Chaos. Very well—that traitor can go with
you. But he would be best warned to tread warily.
The Lords of Chaos have been known to bear mal-
ice . . .'

Rackhir said hoarsely: 'So I have heard, My Lord
Arioch.'

Arioch ignored the archer. 'The man of Phum is
not, after all, important. And if you wish to spare
your cousin's life, so be it. It matters little. Destiny
can contain a few extra threads in her design and still
accomplish her original aims.'

'Very well then,' said Elric. 'Take us from this
place.'

'Where to?'

'Why, to Melniboné, if you please.'

With a smile that was almost tender Arioch
looked down on Elric and a silky hand stroked
Elric's cheek. Arioch had grown to twice his original size. 'Oh, you are surely the sweetest of all my
slaves,' said the Lord of Chaos.

And there was a whirling. There was a sound like
the roar of the sea. There was a dreadful sense of
nausea. And three weary men stood on the floor of
the great throne room in Imrryr. The throne room
was deserted, save that in one corner a black shape,
like smoke, writhed for a moment and then was
gone.

Rackhir crossed the floor and seated himself carefully upon the first step to the Ruby Throne. Yyrkoon and Elric remained where they were, staring
into each other's eyes. Then Elric laughed and
slapped his scabbarded sword. 'Now you must fulfil
your promises to me, cousin. Then I have a proposi-
tion to put to you.'

'It is like a market place,' said Rackhir, leaning on
one elbow and inspecting the feather in his scarlet
hat. 'So many bargains!'

5

The Pale King's Mercy

YYRKOON STEPPED BACK from his sister's bed. He
was worn and his features were drawn and there was
no spirit in him as he said: 'It is done.' He turned
away and looked through the window at the towers
of Imrryr, at the harbour where the returned golden
battle-barges rode at anchor, together with the ship
which had been King Straasha's gift to Elric. 'She
will wake in a moment,' added Yyrkoon absently.

Dyvim Tvar and Rackhir the Red Archer looked
inquiringly at Elric who kneeled by the bed, staring
into the face of Cymoril. Her face grew peaceful as
he watched and for one terrible moment he suspected Prince Yyrkoon of tricking him and of kill-
ing Cymoril. But then the eyelids moved and the
eyes opened and she saw him and she smiled. 'Elric?
The dreams . . . You are safe?'

'I am safe, Cymoril. As are you.'

'Yyrkoon . . . ?'

'He woke you.'

'But you swore to slay him . . .'

'I was as much subject to sorcery as you. My

mind was confused. It is still confused where some matters are concerned. But Yyrkoon is changed now. I defeated him. He does not doubt my power. He no longer lusts to usurp me.'

'You are merciful, Elric.' She brushed raven hair from her face.

Elric exchanged a glance with Rackhir.

'It might not be mercy which moves me,' said Elric. 'It might merely be a sense of fellowship with Yyrkoon.'

'Fellowship? Surely you cannot feel . . . ?'

'We are both mortal. We were both victims of a game played between the Lords of the Higher Worlds. My loyalty must, finally, be to my own kind—and that is why I ceased to hate Yyrkoon.'

'And that is mercy,' said Cymoril.

Yyrkoon walked towards the door. 'May I leave, my lord emperor?'

Elric thought he detected a strange light in his defeated cousin's eyes. But perhaps it was only humility or despair. He nodded. Yyrkoon went from the room, closing the door softly.

Dyvim Tvar said: 'Trust Yyrkoon not at all, Elric. He will betray you again.' The Lord of the Dragon Caves was troubled.

'No,' said Elric. 'If he does not fear me, he fears the sword I now carry.'

'And you should fear that sword,' said Dyvim Tvar.

'No,' said Elric. 'I am the master of the sword.'

Dyvim Tvar made to speak again but then shook his head almost sorrowfully, bowed and, together with Rackhir the Red Archer, left Elric and Cymoril alone.

Cymoril took Elric in her arms. They kissed. They wept.

There were celebrations in Melniboné for a week.

Now almost all the ships and men and dragons were home. And Elric was home, having proved his right to rule so well that all his strange quirks of character (this 'mercy' of his was perhaps the strangest) were accepted by the populace.

In the throne room there was a ball and it was the most lavish ball any of the courtiers had ever known. Elric danced with Cymoril, taking a full part in the activities. Only Yyrkoon did not dance, preferring to remain in a quiet corner below the gallery of the music-slaves, ignored by the guests. Rackhir the Red Archer danced with several Melnibonéan ladies and made assignations with them all, for he was a hero now in Melniboné. Dyvim Tvar danced, too, though his eyes were often brooding when they fell upon Prince Yyrkoon.

And later, when people ate, Elric spoke to Cymoril as they sat together on the dais of the Ruby Throne.

'Would you be empress, Cymoril?'

'You know I will marry you, Elric. We have both known that for many a year, have we not?'

'So you would be my wife?'

'Aye.' She laughed for she thought he joked.

'And not be empress? For a year at least?'

'What mean you, my lord.'

'I must go away from Melniboné, Cymoril, for a year. What I have learned in recent months has made me want to travel the Young Kingdoms—see how other nations conduct their affairs. For I think Melniboné must change if she is to survive. She could become a great force for good in the world, for she still has much power.'

'For good?' Cymoril was surprised and there was a little alarm in her voice, too. 'Melniboné has never stood for good or for evil, but for herself and the satisfaction of her desires.'

'I would see that changed.'

'You intend to alter everything?'

'I intend to travel the world and then decide if there is any point to such a decision. The Lords of the Higher Worlds have ambitions in our world. Though they have given me aid, of late, I fear them. I should like to see if it is possible for men to rule their own affairs.'

'And you will go?' There were tears in her eyes. 'When?'

'Tomorrow—when Rackhir leaves. We will take King Straasha's ship and make for the Isle of the Purple Towns where Rackhir has friends. Will you come?'

'I cannot imagine—I cannot. Oh, Elric, why spoil this happiness we now have?'

'Because I feel that the happiness cannot last unless we know completely what we are.'

She frowned. 'Then you must discover that, if that is what you wish,' she said slowly. 'But it is for you to discover alone, Elric, for I have no such desire. You must go by yourself into those barbarian lands.'

'You will not accompany me?'

'It is not possible. I—I am Melnibonéan . . .' She sighed. 'I love you, Elric.'

'And I you, Cymoril.'

'Then we shall be married when you return. In a year.'

Elric was full of sorrow, but he knew that his decision was correct. If he did not leave, he would grow restless soon enough and if he grew restless he might come to regard Cymoril as an enemy, someone who had trapped him.

'Then you must rule as empress until I return,' he said.

'No, Elric I cannot take that responsibility.'

'Then, who . . . ? Dyvim Tvar . . .'

'I know Dyvim Tvar. He will not take such power.

Magum Colim, perhaps . . .'

'No.'

'Then you must stay, Elric.'

But Elric's gaze had travelled through the crowd in the throne room below. It stopped when it reached a lonely figure seated by itself under the gallery of the music-slaves. And Elric smiled ironically and said:

'Then it must be Yyrkoon.'

Cymoril was horrified. 'No, Elric. He will abuse any power . . .'

'Not now. And it is just. He is the only one who wanted to be emperor. Now he can rule as emperor for a year in my stead. If he rules well, I may consider abdicating in his favour. If he rules badly, it will prove, once and for all, that his ambitions were misguided.'

'Elric,' said Cymoril. 'I love you. But you are a fool—a criminal, if you trust Yyrkoon again.'

'No,' he said evenly. 'I am not a fool. All I am is Elric. I cannot help that, Cymoril.'

'It is Elric that I love!' she cried. 'But Elric is doomed. We are all doomed unless you remain here now.'

'I cannot. Because I love you, Cymoril, I cannot.'

She stood up. She was weeping. She was lost.

'And I am Cymoril,' she said. 'You will destroy us both.' Her voice softened and she stroked his hair. 'You will destroy us, Elric.'

'No,' he said. 'I will build something that will be better. I will discover things. When I return we shall marry and we shall live long and we shall be happy, Cymoril.'

And now, Elric had told three lies. The first concerned his cousin Yyrkoon. The second concerned the Black Sword. The third concerned Cymoril. And upon those three lies was Elric's destiny to be built, for it is only about things which concern us

most profoundly that we lie clearly and with profound conviction.

EPILOGUE

THERE WAS A port called Menii which was one of the humblest and friendliest of the Purple Towns. Like the others on the isle it was built mainly of the purple stone which gave the towns their name. And there were red roofs on the houses and there were bright-sailed boats of all kinds in the harbour as Elric and Rackhir the Red Archer came ashore in the early morning when just a few sailors were beginning to make their way down to their ships.

King Straasha's lovely ship lay some way out beyond the harbour wall. They had used a small boat to cross the water between it and the town. They turned and looked back at the ship. They had sailed it themselves, without crew, and the ship had sailed well.

'So, I must seek peace and mythic Tanelorn,' said Rackhir, with a certain amount of self-mockery. He stretched and yawned and the bow and the quiver danced on his back.

Elric was dressed in simple costume that might have marked any soldier-of-fortune of the Young Kingdoms. He looked fit and relaxed. He smiled into the sun. The only remarkable thing about his garb was the great, black runesword at his side. Since he had donned the sword, he had needed no drugs to sustain him at all.

'And I must seek knowledge in the lands I find marked upon my map,' said Elric. 'I must learn and I must carry what I learn back to Melniboné at the end of a year. I wish that Cymoril had accompanied me, but I understand her reluctance.'

'You will go back?' Rackhir said. 'When a year is over?'

'She will draw me back!' Elric laughed. 'My only fear is that I will weaken and return before my quest is finished.'

'I should like to come with you,' said Rackhir, 'for I have travelled in most lands and would be as good a guide as I was in the netherworld. But I am sworn to find Tanelorn, for all I know it does not really exist.'

'I hope that you find it, Warrior Priest of Phum,' said Elric.

'I shall never be that again,' said Rackhir. Then his eyes widened a little. 'Why, look—your ship!'

And Elric looked and saw the ship that had once been called The Ship Which Sails Over Land and Sea, and he saw that slowly it was sinking. King Straasha was taking it back.

'The elementals are friends, at least,' he said. 'But I fear their power wanes as the power of Melniboné wanes. For all that we of the Dragon Isle are considered evil by the folk of the Young Kingdoms, we share much in common with the spirits of Air, Earth, Fire and Water.'

Rackhir said, as the masts of the ship disappeared beneath the waves: 'I envy you those friends, Elric. You may trust them.'

'Aye.'

Rackhir looked at the runesword hanging on

Elric's hip. 'But you would be wise to trust nothing else,' he added.

Elric laughed. 'Fear not for me, Rackhir, for I am my own master—for a year at least. And I am master of this sword now!'

The sword seemed to stir at his side and he took firm hold of its grip and slapped Rackhir on the back and he laughed and shook his white hair so that it drifted in the air and he lifted his strange, red eyes to the sky and he said:

'I shall be a new man when I return to Melniboné.'

277